And the Winner Is . . .

The five prom queen candidates were all parading onstage in their gorgeous prom dresses. All the dresses looked alike. They were all bright red.

The principal was standing at the microphone. He held a small white envelope in his left hand. Next to him stood the student council president. She was holding the queen's crown and scepter.

"And now," said the principal, "this year's winner and Shadyside's prom queen . . . "

He ripped open the envelope. All the kids at the prom had stopped dancing and turned to look.

All eyes were on the prom queens now, including the principal's. What he saw was so horrifying that he never announced the winner.

On the stage, one by one, the prom queens slowly turned to face the audience.

As they turned, screams rang out through the auditorium.

Books by R. L. Stine

Fear Street

THE NEW GIRL
THE SURPRISE PARTY
THE OVERNIGHT
MISSING
THE WRONG NUMBER
THE SLEEPWALKER
HAUNTED
HALLOWEEN PARTY
THE STEPSISTER
SKI WEEKEND
THE FIRE GAME
LIGHTS OUT
THE SECRET BEDROOM
THE KNIFE
PROM QUEEN
FIRST DATE
THE BEST FRIEND
THE CHEATER
SUNBURN
THE NEW BOY
THE DARE
BAD DREAMS
DOUBLE DATE
THE THRILL CLUB
ONE EVIL SUMMER

Fear Street Super Chiller

PARTY SUMMER
SILENT NIGHT
GOODNIGHT KISS
BROKEN HEARTS
SILENT NIGHT 2
THE DEAD LIFEGUARD

The Fear Street Saga

THE BETRAYAL
THE SECRET
THE BURNING

Fear Street Cheerleaders

THE FIRST EVIL
THE SECOND EVIL
THE THIRD EVIL

99 Fear Street: The House of Evil

THE FIRST HORROR
THE SECOND HORROR
THE THIRD HORROR

Other Novels

HOW I BROKE UP WITH ERNIE
PHONE CALLS
CURTAINS
BROKEN DATE

Available from ARCHWAY Paperbacks

FEAR STREET®
R.L. STINE

The Prom Queen

CHARDON LIBRARY

AN ARCHWAY PAPERBACK
Published by POCKET BOOKS

New York   London   Toronto   Sydney   Tokyo   Singapore

AN ARCHWAY PAPERBACK *Original*

An Archway Paperback published by
POCKET BOOKS, a division of Simon & Schuster Inc.
1230 Avenue of the Americas, New York, NY 10020

ISBN: 0-671-72485-1

First Archway Paperback printing March 1992

10   9

Cover art by Bill Schmidt

Printed in the U.S.A.

IL 6+

chapter

1

We couldn't stop talking about the killer. We tried to shut him out of our minds. But then one of us would remember and say something, and the talk would start all over again.

We were all nervous. Not that any of us admitted it. No, we acted like it was all some big joke. But we were nervous, believe me. Because the murder took place so nearby. Because the victim was a girl our age—a girl just like us.

"Look at it this way," Dawn was saying as she buttoned up her white silk blouse. "At least the girl won't have to worry about finding a date for the prom."

"You're disgusting," I told her.

"For sure," Rachel agreed.

It was after my gym class on Tuesday. The locker

room was crowded with girls all trying to get dressed in a hurry for the prom assembly. The hot and steamy air was filled with shrieks and laughter.

I put my left foot up on the wooden bench between Dawn and Rachel, who was wriggling into a pair of black denims, and hurriedly tied my sneaker. "Did you see the thing on the morning news?" I asked them.

Rachel shook her head. Dawn answered, "About the murder?"

"Yeah. They showed the police tramping around in the Fear Street woods searching for clues. And they showed the muddy ravine where the hiker had found the body. Finally they showed the girl zipped up in a blue body bag."

"Yuck!" Dawn gagged.

"They also showed a blurry black-and-white photo of the girl—she had a really sweet smile. They said she was stabbed sixteen times."

"Well, she's not smiling anymore," quipped Dawn bitterly.

Dawn had been making jokes like that since we'd heard about the murder. I figured it was her way of dealing with it. She was usually pretty good at hiding her emotions.

Rachel glowered at her. "I just don't think it's funny."

"Lighten up," Dawn replied sharply. "It's not like it was your sister or something. It's some girl nobody knows."

"I called my cousin Jackie at lunch," Rachel answered quietly. "She lives in Waynesbridge. She says she knew her."

Dawn and I both spoke at once. "She knew her?" "Why didn't you tell us?" "What did she say?" "How well did she know her?"

"*Very* well," Rachel said, answering only my last question. "They were like best buddies. Jackie was all broken up, a total mess."

Rachel had been brushing her straight red hair in long hard strokes, but abruptly stopped. Her face became pale. "I can't believe this really happened right here in Shadyside. I mean, it's so horrible."

"Does your cousin Jackie have any idea who might have done it?" Dawn asked.

Rachel shook her head. "No. She says Stacy was just a nice kid who everybody liked. The police talked to Jackie, but she was too upset to think clearly. She couldn't tell them a thing."

She dropped her hairbrush into her backpack and zipped it shut. "I live on Fear Street, you know, and they found the body only a block from my house. I keep thinking it could have been me. I could have been the one they found."

"Well, it couldn't have been me," insisted Dawn as she finished applying her lip gloss. "With all the weird stuff that goes on there, I wouldn't be caught *dead* in the Fear Street woods." She realized what she had said and burst out laughing.

"Yeah?" I said. "Well, this morning they interviewed this cop on TV. And he said that the murderer must have staked out Stacy's house. He thinks this psycho waited until she was all alone, and then . . ."

I looked up and paused just to tease my friends.

"And then?" Dawn demanded.

"He murdered her in her bedroom."

Dawn's mouth fell open in a frightened little *O*. "I've always hated being alone in my house," she confided.

"Somehow I don't think this is going to help you get over your problem," I told her.

Dawn stared blankly at me for a moment. Just a moment. Then she shrieked, clutched her head, and continued to yell at the top of her lungs. Her fake outburst earned her a chorus of laughter from the girls who were left in the locker room.

On the other side of the room Shari Paulsen held up an imaginary knife and started stabbing the air and making that weird sound from *Psycho*. You know the sound—the one they play whenever Anthony Perkins is stabbing somebody—*Eee! Eee! Eee!*

Then Shari marched around the locker room like a crazed zombie, pretending to stab everyone in sight. There was a lot of screaming.

It wasn't really funny, but we laughed anyway. I mean, how should someone react when something horrible happens so close to home? Maybe kidding around like that helps. I don't know.

The girl at the end of our row slammed her locker door shut and hurried out. Dawn jumped at the sound, as if someone had fired a gun. "Okay," she said, "we've got to stop talking about this. I'm starting to freak out."

"Then I guess you don't want to hear the worst thing," I said.

Dawn and Rachel both groaned. "Worse than being stabbed sixteen times?" Dawn asked. "What happened? She was run over by a truck?"

"I thought you didn't want to know any more," I said.

"What? What? What?" she begged.

I continued. "The police said this killing is just like the killing of that girl in Durham last week."

Durham was about an hour's drive from Shadyside. But right then that didn't seem very far at all.

"So?" Dawn said. "What does that mean?"

"Well," I said, "it means there's a good chance this is the work of a serial killer."

"A serial killer . . ." murmured Rachel. "That does it, I'm going to make my parents buy a dog." She stuffed her feet into a pair of torn running shoes. "I mean, we don't even have a burglar alarm at our house."

It was true—Rachel's parents were pretty poor compared to the rest of ours. I doubted that they could swing for an alarm system, even with a serial killer on the loose.

The bell for next period jangled loudly. There was a groan from the few girls still left in the locker room.

"Come on, you two," Dawn said. "Hurry up." She stood admiring her face in the mirror and made several sexy faces. "I know what we should talk about instead of the murder," she said. "Who should I go to the prom with?" She proceeded to name four of the most popular guys at Shadyside High.

"They *all* asked you?" exclaimed Rachel, astonished.

"Already?" I chimed in. "The prom is still five weeks away."

"Well," Dawn said, "none of them has asked me *yet*. But they will. Believe me."

We were the last ones out of the locker room. The hallways were empty, a sure sign we were late for assembly. We started to run, our sneakers squeaking on the tile floor.

"What about you?" Rachel asked me as we tore down the hallway. "You have a date yet?"

I shook my head no.

I would have had a date. If it wasn't for the United States Army. I'm serious. For over a year I'd been dating Kevin McCormack. Then his father, an army major, got transferred to Alabama.

Kevin's family moved in January. Since then I'd been dating him long distance, by mail. We'd talked on the phone a lot at first, but when my dad got the phone bill, he put an end to that.

So far Major McCormack wouldn't give Kev permission to come back to Shadyside for the prom. Kevin's dad felt it was important for Kevin to get "acclimated to his new home base." Those were the exact words he used, according to Kevin. I believed it. His dad always talked army talk.

"Tell your father he's a Major Bummer," I had written back. Pretty clever, don't you think?

Dawn pulled open the heavy doors to the auditorium. A few heads in the back rows turned to stare at us.

Up on stage Miss Ryan had already begun making announcements. Mr. Abner was standing near the back doors. He caught my eye and glared as we took seats in the back row.

"Mrs. Bartlett has asked me to announce that this week you can return overdue library books without paying fines," Miss Ryan was saying. "So I hope you'll all take advantage of this special opportunity. If you've got overdue library books, please bring them in."

She rustled through ner notes. "Now we can get on to the main business of this assembly, which is to announce our five prom queen candidates."

This news was greeted with applause and a few catcalls from some of the guys. Miss Ryan stared out over the microphone until she had silence. Then she turned toward our principal, who was waiting onstage a few steps behind her. "Mr. Sewall?"

Mr. Sewall was short, pudgy, and bald. He looked kind of like a character from "Sesame Street," so we nicknamed him the Muppet.

He stepped up to the mike, holding a white index

card in his hand. All at once I felt a rush of excitement. I knew it was uncool of me, but I was really into the prom. A lot of my friends were.

We seniors were the only ones allowed to vote. I had voted for Rachel. Rachel wasn't the most popular girl in the class or anything, but that was mainly because she was so shy. Well, I guess it was also because she had a bitter streak in her, about being poor and all. But once you got to know her, she was really sweet and a good friend. Maybe being elected prom queen would help her out of her shell.

Not much chance of her winning, though.

"Before we begin," the Muppet said, "I'd like to say a few words about the tragedy that occurred in the Shadyside area yesterday."

Rachel and I exchanged glances. Dawn put her finger in her mouth and mimed gagging.

"I hope," began Mr. Sewall, "we *all* hope, that the police catch this killer as soon as possible. In the meantime, I don't want anyone to panic. I do think that all girls should be specially careful for a while."

"Great way to keep people from panicking," whispered Dawn.

"Okay," the principal continued. "Now on with the show." He chuckled as if he had told the greatest joke in the world.

"The votes are in." He waved the card. "As you know, the top five vote-getters become nominees for prom queen. What I'd like to do is read off the names of the five winners and ask them to come forward and join me on the stage.

"I'm going to do this alphabetically." He smiled, glanced down his card, then looked back up, letting the suspense build. Then finally he said, "Elizabeth McVay."

For a moment I had absolutely no reaction. I didn't recognize my own name!

Dawn started slapping me on the back and yelling, "Way to go, Lizzy!"

I nearly tripped on my way up the aisle, and since we had been sitting in the back, I had a long way to go. I felt a little dizzy.

When I got onstage, Mr. Sewall shook my hand.

I wished I'd remembered the assembly that day. I was wearing a ratty pair of jeans and my dad's old blue cotton workshirt. My long, curly hair was still wet from the locker-room shower.

My hair is light brown at best—honey brown, my mom always calls it. But when it's wet, it's just plain brown. I brushed my wispy bangs out of my eyes. They fell right back down.

The Muppet leaned back over the mike and said, "Our second prom queen nominee is . . . Simone Perry."

There was a big burst of applause. Simone stood up and started sidestepping between rows toward the aisle.

Simone was dressed in her flashiest outfit—a silky black blouse and a leather skirt. I guessed that she'd remembered there was an assembly that day.

As she headed toward the stage, she kept tossing back her long dark hair with a dramatic shake of her head.

"Congratulations," I whispered when she took her place next to me.

"Thanks," she said, whispering back.

I wasn't surprised when she forgot to add, "You too." I liked Simone, but she had a tendency to forget that the whole world didn't revolve around her.

"Elana Potter!" Mr. Sewall announced next.

More applause. Elana stood up with a big smile and walked bouncily up the aisle. She didn't look surprised at all. No wonder. She was one of the most popular girls at Shadyside, as she well knew.

Two more to go. I peered into the back of the hall, where Dawn and Rachel were sitting. I knew Dawn must be freaking. She was probably angry that she hadn't been announced first, even if Mr. Sewall was going by the alphabet.

"Dawn Rodgers!"

Dawn gave a whoop and clapped her hands. She wasn't the only one clapping. In fact, she was getting the most applause so far.

She pumped her fist in the air as she headed toward the stage. That got another round of applause. It was the gesture she always used after she scored an important point in a tennis match. Dawn was the girls' team captain.

"And last but not least"—Mr. Sewall glanced at the card—"Rachel West!"

Dawn was a hard act to follow. The applause for Rachel was less than thunderous. I did what I could and clapped until my palms hurt.

Rachel didn't seem to mind that she didn't get the most applause. She was smiling and blushing almost the color of her red hair as she joined me onstage.

"Now, as you all know, the prom is fast approaching—just five weeks away," the Muppet continued.

Dawn clapped her hands and enthusiastically cried, "All right!"

"But what you seniors don't know," said the Muppet, "is that as a special treat, I've been able to rent the newly refurbished Halsey Manor House."

He waited for applause. It never came. We all knew the Halsey Manor House was right in the middle of the Fear Street woods—the place where the murdered Stacy had just been found.

He went on, "That should make for quite a party, don't you think?"

The Fear Street woods. Right then it didn't sound like a place I'd want to go, much less go dancing.

Maybe by the end of May it would seem like a good place for the prom. Maybe, but I doubted it.

As Mr. Sewall went on with his speech, I glanced at the other girls onstage. I knew these girls so well that I bet I knew what each one of them was thinking.

It was a game I liked to play sometimes. Mr.

Meade, my English teacher the year before, had taught it to us. He said it was a good game for writers to play. I hadn't written much besides long letters to Kevin in Alabama. But I wanted to write someday.

I started with Simone. Simone was the star of our drama club, and she looked the part. She was tall, dark, and, well, dramatic looking. She was also very insecure, which I guess showed she was meant to be an actress!

She was crazy about her boyfriend, Justin. And more than a little bit possessive. In fact, she was staring at him right then. I could tell by following her gaze out into the audience.

I decided what she was thinking was: Who is Justin talking to? And why isn't he paying attention to me?

Next I focused on Elana. Elana was very pretty in a delicate, old-fashioned way, and she knew how to dress to bring it out. Right then, for instance, she had on a white frilly blouse and a dark green wraparound skirt. She was smiling, showing off a row of perfect white teeth. She was like someone you'd see on a TV commercial.

Everything came easily to Elana. Always had. She got straight A's without seeming to, and her family had oodles of money, so she got whatever she wanted. She was so happy and friendly, though, that it was hard to hold it against her.

What was she thinking right then? Boy, being

nominated sure is fun. Maybe someday I'll be nominated President of the United States!

When I made contact with Dawn, she nodded at me, her blue eyes gleaming. I stared at her for a moment, admiring her tan.

We'd been going through our usual end-of-April rainy spell. But Dawn always had a tan, no matter what the weather. Her long, wavy blond hair gleamed shiny and golden, as if she'd been out in the sun for hours.

She probably had. Dawn was an ace at tennis and at every other sport. Including boys.

I knew what she was thinking. It was in her eyes. I'm going to win!

"Now," the Muppet was saying, "I know each of you would love to be elected prom queen. And this year there's even more reason to want to win—the queen will receive a special three-thousand-dollar scholarship, donated by Gary Brandt's father at Brandt Chevrolet."

As he made this announcement, I happened to be looking to my left—at Rachel. I could see her emerald eyes light up when he made that announcement. It was like in a cartoon when dollar signs appear in somebody's eyes. The money would mean a lot to Rachel, I knew. Hey, I wouldn't have minded three thousand dollars myself.

As I've already mentioned, Rachel's family was kind of poor, at least compared to the rest of ours. Rachel was the only kid I knew who *had* to work after school. It got her frustrated because it took time away from her schoolwork, and her grades were suffering as a result. She said she might not be able to go to college.

I'd often thought that was why she was so shy—feeling as if she wasn't as good as the rest of us. She didn't even know how pretty she was.

Mr. Sewall's next words brought me back to the present. "School dismissed!"

There was the usual end-of-the-day pandemonium. People were shouting congratulations to me and the other nominees. Before I could get off the stage, Dawn grabbed me by the arm.

"I'm going to win," she whispered fiercely in my ear. "I can just feel it."

I smiled at her. Over the years I'd gotten used to Dawn's competitive boasting. It was as if she thought life was a game, and she had to psych everyone out so she'd win.

As I was going down the stage steps, Simone brushed past me and almost knocked me over. I watched as she made her way through the crowd toward Justin.

She seemed pretty angry. And Justin had an embarrassed grin on his face.

"Uh, Lizzy?"

It was Rachel. With that quiet voice of hers, I almost didn't hear her. "Do you want to come over and study tonight?" she asked.

"I'd like to," I said genuinely. "But my parents

told me this morning they want me home early and they don't want me going out after dark."

I'm an only child. Maybe that's why my mom and dad have always been so overprotective. But this time I didn't mind it. With a killer on the loose, being overly protected sounded just great.

I could still see Simone arguing heatedly with Justin. Amazing. How much trouble could he get into during one assembly? Justin uttered an exasperated cry, threw his hands up in the air, and hurried out.

"I can't believe I was nominated," Rachel said.

"Why not?" I replied. "You deserve it."

"I know," she cracked. "I just didn't know anyone *else* knew!"

I laughed as Elana walked up to us. Her perfect little apple cheeks were flushed red with excitement; she resembled a porcelain doll.

"It's time to celebrate," she said. "How about we all go to Pete's Pizza? I'm driving. I've got the Mercedes today!"

Rachel flashed a broad smile. She always got a thrill at being included in any group outing.

"Way to go, Elana!" Brad Coleman said, clapping her on the back as he hurried past. Anything for a chance to touch her, I thought.

Smiling a perfect smile, Elana called back her thanks. She tossed her short blond hair. "Simone!"

Simone was about twenty yards away, an unhappy scowl on her face. "I can't believe it," she grumbled, walking over to us. "During the assembly I saw Justin coming on to Meg Dalton. If he goes out with her behind my back, I'll kill him."

It's funny. That silly threat was the first thing that flashed through my mind two days later when we learned that Simone had disappeared.

chapter
2

"*T*his is so cool!" Elana yelled over the noise of the car radio, which was cranked up all the way. "I mean, trying to guess which of us will be prom queen."

We had all piled into Elana's parents' silver Mercedes and were headed for Pete's Pizza. I was in the backseat between Rachel and Simone. Dawn was in the front, changing the radio stations non-stop.

"Dawn, turn that down!" screeched Simone, staring into a green folder in her lap. "I'm trying to learn my lines."

For the drama club's spring production, Robbie Barron was directing *The Sound of Music*. The show would be performed on the Friday night of prom weekend, to kick off our spring festival.

Simone was playing Maria Von Trapp, of course. She always was the star. Even though she didn't make a very convincing nun.

Dawn clicked off the radio and said, "You're right, Elana, one of us is going to be prom queen, but I'm the only one who knows who. Me."

Simone leaned forward. "You'll win for humility, that's for sure," she said sarcastically.

"*If* I wanted to win a humility contest, I *could* win it," Dawn said. "No one can beat me at anything."

I glanced at Rachel, and she rolled her eyes.

Elana pulled into the Division Street Mall and glided into a parking space near the restaurant. "Lock up," she told us, hopping out.

"Sure," muttered Rachel as she got out of the car. "We wouldn't want the car to be stolen. It'd be at least a day before her dad could buy another one."

I laughed quietly. I didn't know how else to react to Rachel's bitterness.

I had to admit I was feeling good. Really happy. But then Rachel brought up the murder again.

The restaurant was packed. We had trouble finding a table for five. When we found one, way in the back, it took hours for a waitress to appear to take our order.

The pizza had finally arrived and we were grabbing for slices when Rachel said, "What if the mayor gives us an early curfew because of the killer?"

Everyone groaned. "Seriously," Rachel insisted. "What if we can't have the prom because of that dead girl—Stacy?"

"Gee, Rachel," Dawn said, "you were criticizing me for not being sensitive. I mean, a girl gets murdered, and all you can think about is the prom."

Rachel blushed. "That's not what I meant," she muttered. "I mean, I— Oh, never mind."

Simone had a thoughtful expression on her face. I asked her what she was thinking.

"About my parents," she replied, frowning. Here I'm the star of this play, and I bet they won't come to see me." She dropped her pizza slice onto her plate. "When I tell them about being a prom queen candidate, they won't even say a word."

"Simone," I chided her. "You know they care. They're just busy, that's all."

"The only thing I keep thinking about is this killer. Isn't there anything we can do to protect ourselves from this psychopath?" Elana asked, obsessing about the killer.

I said, "Maybe we could all disguise ourselves as guys."

Simone immediately took up my idea. She lowered her voice. "Hey, there aren't any young high school girls here, Mr. Serial Killer," she growled. "You must have the wrong house."

She rubbed her nose roughly like a guy would and coughed as if to spit. By then we were all laughing. Whenever I thought Simone was too self-centered to bother with, she acted funny. And then I forgave her.

"You know what?" Dawn said. "I don't think I'm going to sleep so hot tonight, either."

"You'll sleep better than I will," Rachel told her. "I'm the one who lives on Fear Street—remember?"

Just then two hands closed around her neck.

"Gotcha," a male voice said.

It was Gideon Miller, Rachel's boyfriend.

"Not funny!" Rachel cried, but she smiled up at him anyway.

"Were you girls talking about me?" Gideon asked, grinning.

"No. Actually," said Dawn, "we were talking about the killer."

"That's cheerful," Gideon said dryly, rolling his eyes. "Hey—is Rachel going to win the three thousand dollars?" he asked and put his hands on her shoulders.

"What do you care?" Rachel asked. "If I win, you don't think I'd share it with you—do you? Even you aren't *that* egotistical."

Gideon laughed. "Ooh—big word. Big word! Have you been studying your vocabulary list today?" He waved to the guys he was with, who were waiting for him just inside the glass doors. "No, I just thought if you won, maybe you'd take me to a movie or something."

"Maybe," Rachel teased.

"Gotta go," Gideon said. He gave Rachel's shoulders a squeeze and headed off to join his friends.

"What were we talking about?" Simone asked, pulling all the pepperoni off her slice and stuffing it into her mouth.

"The killer," Rachel replied, her eyes following Gideon.

"Please—" Elana wiped her mouth primly with a napkin—"enough talking about this killer business. I mean it."

"All right," Dawn said. "We'll talk about something else. I know—let's talk about the prom and about how I'm going to be elected queen."

"I've got a better idea. What about the two-minute speeches we have to give to the entire school?" Elana suggested. "Have any of you thought about them?"

Just then I had an idea. It was kind of a variation on Mr. Meade's game. "Let's do each other's speeches," I said. Everyone's expression was blank. "It'll be fun," I said, explaining. "Right now."

"All right," Simone said. "I'll do Dawn."

She tilted her head back and put her hair behind her ears the way Dawn wore hers. She stuck her jaw out as Dawn did when she was feeling competitive, which was just about always.

It was amazing. With just a few simple gestures, Simone had transformed herself into Dawn! Everyone began to laugh, Dawn the loudest, clapping her hands as if she really found Simone amusing. I knew she hated it, though.

"Hi," Simone began. "My name's Dawn Rodgers. Yeah!" She pumped her first in the air in victory.

"Right on!" shouted some jocks at a nearby table.

Dawn had a big grin on her face, but she was blushing. She had to be blushing pretty hard to see it through her tan.

"Anyway," continued Simone. "Let's face it, I'm your next prom queen."

We all clapped. Simone acknowledged the applause by pumping her fist again. Laughing harder, Dawn said, "Okay, my turn, I'll—" But Simone kept going.

"Now, I know there are four other candidates," Simone continued. "But as you all know, I'm number one in everything I do, so—"

"Okay." Dawn jumped up, her eyes flashing. "My turn. Here's Simone's speech."

I was beginning to think this wasn't such a bright idea after all.

"But I'm not finished yet," Simone said.

"My name's Simone Perry," Dawn said, ignoring her. She tossed her hair back the way Simone always did. "Gee, I have so many people to thank for winning this Oscar for best actress—oops. What am I saying? I mean, for winning prom queen."

Now it was Simone's turn to pretend to be enjoying it.

"I'd just like to say that I'm such a sensitive artist," cooed Dawn, "that I'm the only one capable of playing the role of a queen."

She took a deep bow, then sat down and smiled sweetly at Simone. "How did I do?"

"You know," I said, "maybe we should—"

"My name is Rachel West," said Elana, standing up.

Oh, no, I thought. Elana—please.

"And, uh . . ." Elana imitated Rachel's slow way of talking. "Uh . . . well, I'm kinda poor."

"Ha-ha," said Rachel. I could see she had been stung, but she had a big grin plastered across her face. Simone was laughing as Elana went on. "I—I, uh, wanted to prepare a speech, but I couldn't afford it!"

Rachel let out a loud, extra-fake guffaw. "Gee, that's *so* funny, I almost forgot to laugh."

"Glad you liked it," Elana responded.

"I really did." Rachel grinned. I could see she was trying to think of something cutting to say, but she couldn't, so she just sat there, smiling.

"Do Elana's speech," Simone coaxed.

"Simone," I said, "I think this is getting out of—"

"All right," Rachel said. "I will." She stood up. "My name's Elana Potter. It doesn't matter if I'm prom queen or not. If I lose, my father will just send me on a trip to Europe until I'm feeling all better."

She flipped one side of her hair and lolled her head around the way Elana always did. Simone and Dawn were hysterical. Elana's smile was frozen on her face.

"No, but seriously, if there's anyone here who's thinking of *not* voting for me"—Rachel imitated Elana's flirty laugh—"I'll pay you a thousand dollars to change your mind."

Elana clapped loudly—twice. "Not bad," she said, "but I don't have to buy anyone's vote. If you heard the applause today, you'd know that."

"Well, you couldn't buy mine," Rachel shot back, sitting down again.

For a long moment no one said a thing. You could tell that everyone had gone just a little bit too far. Honesty is a good policy—but not *too much* honesty.

"Great game, Lizzy," Dawn finally said. "Now someone's got to do you."

"That's okay. Don't do me any favors."

"No way," Dawn persisted. "Everybody plays. Right, Simone?"

But Simone wasn't listening. She was staring past us, toward the front window of the restaurant.

"Simone?" I said.

Simone's face had gone white.

"Oh, no," she mumbled. She stood up fast, knocking over my Sprite. The soda splashed all over Dawn and me. We both jumped out of our seats at the same time.

"Oh, no," Simone repeated. *"No!"*

She had a look of total horror on her face. She screamed, "No! Stop!"

And then raced out of the restaurant.

chapter
3

We were all on our feet now, staring out the window at Simone. We saw right away why she was so upset.

Just outside Pete's is a big indoor fountain. Standing beside the fountain was her boyfriend, Justin.

He was standing very close to a tall, hot-looking blond girl—Vanessa Hartley.

We watched as Simone approached them. We could see her call out to Justin, then fling her arm around his neck. It wasn't the most affectionate gesture I had even seen.

"She's not too possessive or anything," I cracked, watching Justin squirm. He moved away from Simone and nearly fell over backward into the fountain.

"It figures," said Dawn. "If Simone is screaming, it's nothing important."

"She forgets she's not on stage all the time," agreed Rachel, sitting back down.

"She's jealous of anyone who even looks at Justin," said Elana.

I was still watching the scene out the window. Vanessa had taken off in a hurry. Justin had his arm around Simone now. He was talking to her, those light blue eyes of his flashing close to her face.

"I'd be jealous too," I joked. "Justin is such a babe!"

I wasn't kidding. Without exaggeration, I'd have to say that Justin was the best-looking, coolest, most popular guy at Shadyside High. And as if that wasn't enough, he was also an all-state baseball player and the team captain of the Shadyside Tigers.

Dawn leaned toward us and lowered her voice. "Can you guys keep a secret? Well, I can't any longer." She took a long dramatic pause before saying, "I went out with Justin last week."

Elana's jaw dropped open, which meant she showed us a mouthful of chewed cheese and pepperoni. "You did *what?*" she asked.

"Justin *Stiles?*" I couldn't help exclaiming. "As in, Simone's boyfriend?"

"Hey," Dawn said defensively, "it's not like I tried to steal him away from her. He asked me, so I went." She shrugged. "We had a good time too."

"I'll bet," said Elana, staring wistfully out the window at Justin. "I'd say yes if he asked me. Wouldn't you, Liz?"

"Sure," I agreed. "If he wasn't seeing Simone."

"Oh, what are you, a Girl Scout?" Dawn sneered.

"What about you, Rachel?" Elana asked. "What would you say if Justin asked you out?"

Rachel cracked a tiny smile. "He already asked me," she said.

Elana's jaw dropped open again.

Rachel's smile broadened. "I said yes," she added.

"The hills are alive," sang Robbie Barron, flouncing around the stage, "with the sound of music."

He was surrounded by laughing nuns. They were waiting to rehearse an abbey scene. But Simone hadn't shown up. She was late for the nine hundredth time.

To pass the time Robbie had started doing an imitation of Simone. He was wearing Eva Clarke's black and white hood and was dancing around like a madman. He did look pretty funny, with his thick, black-framed glasses.

When he finished singing, he said, "That'll teach Simone to be late." He looked at his watch and scowled. "I wonder if our little Maria realizes that it's hard to rehearse without the lead?"

"How do you solve a problem like Maria," the kids playing the nuns sang back.

Robbie laughed but not for long. "I know how I'm going to solve the problem—I'm going to wring her neck."

I was there because I was in charge of sets. I wouldn't be caught dead acting in front of an audience. I bet if I did act, that's what I'd be—dead. I'd drop dead from stage fright!

Right then I was standing in the wings painting a flat to look like the wall of the reverend mother's abbey. This week, after the two murders, my over-protective parents let me out of the house at night for play rehearsals only.

"Hey, Lizzy," Robbie called, "do you have *any* idea where your friend Simone might be?"

"Oh, sure," I answered sarcastically. "When she's in trouble, she's *my* friend."

"Come on, don't give me a hard time." Robbie sounded as if he was out of patience. "Do you know where she is or not?"

"No, I don't—sorry."

"Well, this is getting ridiculous," Robbie continued, checking his watch once again. "This is late even for Simone."

It was true—being late was part of Simone's style. No matter what the occasion, she always ran at least half an hour behind.

Two days had passed since the nominations for prom queen were announced. I hadn't seen much of Simone, or any of the other nominees, since that afternoon at Pete's. We hadn't left on the best of terms.

"Maybe she forgot she had rehearsal," offered one of the nuns.

"I reminded her three times today," Robbie answered. "And I yelled at her about being late." He pushed his black-framed glasses back up on his nose. "But still, knowing Simone, it's possible she forgot."

He sighed dramatically and fished some change out of his jeans pocket. "Eva," he said, "would you mind calling Simone's house?"

There was a pay phone outside the principal's office. Eva was gone for several minutes. "No answer," she announced when she returned.

I dropped my paintbrush into the coffee can filled with water and peered out into the house. Justin liked to watch Simone's rehearsals. He was usually slouched in the back row of the auditorium.

Not that night, though.

I stood up. "I'll go look for her," I volunteered. "Maybe she's somewhere around the school."

I jumped off the stage and started wandering through the empty hallways. There weren't many lights on. And there was absolutely nobody around. I don't scare easily. But walking around empty hallways in the dark has never been high on my list of fun things to do.

Where would I be, I asked myself, if I were Simone and I had forgotten about rehearsal?

First I tried the library, but it was locked. Then I headed for the gym downstairs. Sometimes she hung around there waiting for Justin to finish baseball practice.

I opened the door to the stairwell. It sure was dark down there. You'd think they'd keep a few lights on when people were still using the school!

I hesitated for a moment and then went in.

The heavy door shut behind me with a very loud *click.* Suddenly wary, I turned and tried the doorknob.

The door had locked behind me.

I suddenly felt a heaviness in the pit of my stomach. I didn't want to be locked in a stairwell in the dark all night. I prayed that the gym would be open.

I groped my way down the darkened stairs. By the time I got to the bottom, it was just about pitch-dark. I was waving my hands around in front of me in slow motion, trying to feel my way.

As my eyes adjusted to the darkness, I found the door to the gym and turned the knob. Locked.

I'm trapped in here, I thought.

I can't get out.

I—I can't breathe!

No. I could breathe perfectly fine. I scolded myself for overdoing it.

Calm down, Lizzy. Calm down.

My heart was pounding like someone playing on a tom-tom. I began to bang on the locked door with my fists.

"Come on, somebody! Anybody! Let me *out!*"

I pounded for several minutes.

No response.

There was no one else down here.

Simone was probably on stage now, singing her little heart out. Would anyone miss the set designer?

I doubted it.

I tried to tell myself to stay calm, but my fear took over. A wave of terror swept over me.

I had to get out of there. I *had* to.

I started to pound again with all my might. When that didn't work, I started screaming.

I had screamed twice when I heard footsteps approaching on the other side of the gym door.

I stopped screaming. And listened.

I should've felt relieved. But instead, I became more frightened.

My breath caught in my throat. My head was throbbing.

It's the killer, I thought.

He's been hiding in the gym.

He's heard my screams. He knows I'm all alone, trapped in here.

And now he's coming for me.

The footsteps grew louder.

I knew I should run.

But before I could move, the door was pulled open—and I screamed again.

chapter
4

"What's the matter with you? Why are you screaming like that?"

It was Mr. Santucci, the school's maintenance man. He gaped at me, his expression more frightened than mine.

"Why did you come down this way?" he asked, studying my face in the dim light. "This door is locked."

"I-I'm sorry," I stammered. "I was looking for someone."

"There's no one down here," he said, shaking his head. "It's all locked up. You gave me a scare."

I apologized again, feeling like a fool. Why *had* I screamed like that? Why had I let my fear take over?

My heart still pounding, I followed him through the empty gym. Still grumbling, he let me out one of the back doors.

As I was walking through the parking lot, I heard a familiar sound and glanced over toward the lighted tennis courts, which were at the far end of the lot.

The tennis team was practicing. Dawn would be there. Maybe she had seen Simone.

Just as I started toward the courts, the gate in the fence opened and a girl came out. She was too far away for me to see clearly. But I could tell she was tall and carrying a tennis racket in one hand.

I got a little closer and could make out long blond hair. And then I recognized her.

"Dawn!" I called.

She looked up, startled, and barely waved. She opened the door to her mother's red Camaro.

I jogged over to her. She wasn't going to take off without saying hello, was she?

"Dawn!" I called again. "Have you seen Simone?"

She held on to the car door. "Not since school," she called back. She tossed her racket into the car and slid inside.

"Hey! Wait a sec!" I called. She pulled out. I had to jump to the side as Dawn backed up. I waved my arms at her as I ran toward the car.

"What's the rush?" I called as she rolled down her window.

"Sorry," she said. "What's up?"

"I was looking for Simone."

"Yeah, well, like I said, I haven't—"

"Dawn!"

I was only a few feet from her now. Close enough to see her face clearly. It was scratched and bleeding. She looked as if she'd been clawed by a vicious cat.

"It's nothing," Dawn told me, catching my open-mouthed stare.

"What do you mean, it's nothing? You've got—" I was right up beside the car now. "You've got blood all over your tennis whites."

"Oh, well, nothing a little detergent won't—"

"Yeah, but what happened?"

Dawn revved the motor. "I was hitting with Marcie. Turns out she's got this wicked groundstroke. She kept hitting it deeper and deeper. Then I crashed against the stupid fence. It's nothing. It looks a lot worse than it is. But listen, I've got to get home because—ah—well, because I'm late," she finished lamely.

With that she pulled out. I shook my head. It seemed as if she was hiding something, but I had no idea what it could be.

"Lizzy!"

I turned. It was Eva, waving to me from across the parking lot. Standing near her were several of the other cast members. I could see Robbie climb into his car and slam the door.

"I couldn't find her!" I yelled back.

Eva nodded. "Rehearsal is canceled. We have *no* idea where she is."

I suppose I could have gotten Mr. Santucci to open the auditorium and let me finish painting the abbey. But at that point I was no longer in the mood.

I headed for my car, planning to drive straight home. But then I remembered that Simone lived in North Hills, which is near the school. I decided to stop off there on my way. Maybe Simone was home by now.

Her parents' big Lincoln was parked in the driveway. I pulled in behind it. I scooted out and ran up to ring the bell. Mrs. Perry's face appeared beside the drapes, checking to see who was there. Then the door opened.

"Hi, Lizzy," she said distractedly. "How nice to see you." She was wearing her coat. "Please come in."

Mr. Perry walked in from the hall. He was also wearing his coat and was glancing through a pile of mail. "Lizzy McVay!" he exclaimed warmly, as if he had been waiting to see me for weeks. I always thought Mr. Perry was a nice guy.

"Simone is up in her room," Mrs. Perry told me. "At least, I think she is. We just got home, but I saw the light on up there as we drove up."

I smiled and thanked her as I mounted the dark, carpeted front stairs. Nice going, Simone, I thought. She must have totally forgotten about rehearsal.

I slowed down as I neared the top.

It was dark up there except for a strip of light coming from under Simone's door.

"Simone?" I called.

No answer.

Probably listening to music with her headphones on.

I crossed to her door and knocked.

"Simone? It's me, Lizzy. Can I come in?"

Still no answer. I knocked one more time.

Then I opened the door.

And gasped in horror.

The entire room had been torn apart.

The room seemed to tilt. For a moment I felt as if I were about to fall.

The first thing I focused on was Simone's old teddy bear. It lay on the floor near the bed. Its head had been ripped off and white stuffing poked up through its open body. The bear's glassy black eyes stared up at me blankly.

The rest of the room quickly came into focus.

The floor was cluttered with Simone's belongings.

The sheets and bedspread had been pulled off the bed.

A lamp lay broken on its side at the foot of her desk.

Papers were scattered everywhere. One of the

white window curtains had been ripped off its rod.

It looked as if a terrible struggle had taken place.

Uttering a low cry of fright, I started to back away.

But then I saw the most horrifying sight of all.

On the carpet near my feet was a large, dark puddle of blood.

chapter

5

I didn't scream. I came closer to faint-ing. I could smell the blood near my feet and rushed through the room to the open window. I needed fresh air, and fast.

I stuck my head out, gasping for air.

And that's when I saw him.

His figure was illuminated for just an instant by the Perrys' back porch light.

A man.

Running across the backyard into the woods. He was carrying a big gray sack in his arms.

I stared as hard as I could into the darkness. But he ran out of view.

And then I finally began to do what I thought I would have done right away.

I began to scream.

* * *

The next afternoon after school I was back at Simone's house. So were Justin, Robbie, Elana, Dawn, Rachel, and a couple of others. The police had wanted to question all of Simone's good friends.

Even with all the people in the Perrys' living room, the room felt empty. We all missed Simone. No one had seen her since the day before.

The police hadn't arrived yet. No one was saying much. Everyone was pretty scared.

I got up and went into the kitchen. I wanted to see if I could help Mrs. Perry. But mostly I wanted to get out of the living room.

"Oh, Lizzy." Mrs. Perry gave me a brittle smile as I walked in. She was arranging peanut-butter cookies on a plate to serve to all of us. But I could see that her hands were trembling. And her mascara had run slightly. "The police will be here any minute," she told me.

"I'll get that," I said, taking the cookies from her hand.

It was as if she needed something to hold on to to keep her calm. Her hands started to shake even more now. She lifted them to cover her face. "I'm sorry," she said. "It's just that I'm so scared."

I knew what to do when kids started crying or acting scared. I could usually joke them out of it, or hug them, or whatever, till they felt better. Whenever Rachel got really down, for instance, I always used to say, "Your feet stink." It was so stupid that it made her laugh every time.

When adults freaked out, I was totally at a loss though. Obviously I couldn't tell Mrs. Perry that her feet stank.

I just stood there helplessly as Mrs. Perry began to cry. Luckily Mr. Perry came into the kitchen at that moment. He quickly put his arms around his wife.

"Simone's going to be fine," he whispered to her.

"No, she won't," she sobbed.

Mr. Perry tightened his grip around her. "Whoever kidnapped her only wants money. We'll give him whatever he wants, and that'll be the end of it."

I could tell he didn't really believe it. What kind of kidnapper left a puddle of the victim's blood all over the floor?

A killer, that's who.

Like the guy who had killed that girl, Stacy, who was found in the Fear Street woods.

Mr. Perry tried to smile reassuringly at me over his wife's shoulder, but his face was very drawn. There were big, dark bags under his eyes, like a raccoon's circles. "Please just tell everyone the police will be here any minute."

I headed back into the living room.

All the kids stared at me when I went into the room, as if they were hoping I might be Simone.

I shrugged. "They say the cops'll be here any minute."

As if on cue the doorbell rang.

Two police officers were standing on the front

41

porch. Mr. Perry hurried in from the kitchen. His face lit up when he saw them. "Any news?" he asked hopefully.

One of the officers, a tall, lanky guy, shook his head. The other one—a short, dark-haired woman —frowned. Mr. Perry's face fell.

He showed them into the living room and introduced them to all of us. Then he said, "I'll get my wife," and left.

"I really appreciate you taking the time to talk with us," Officer Jackson, the tall, lanky one, told the large group. He looked almost as worried as the Perrys.

"Do you really think it's a kidnapping?" Dawn asked him.

Officer Jackson shrugged his narrow shoulders.

I could hear Mrs. Perry blowing her nose in the kitchen.

"We hope so," Officer Barnett offered with a tight little smile. "But we also have to be prepared for—"

"For the worst," Officer Jackson finished her sentence. "Right now we've got several officers out combing the Fear Street woods."

We all stared at one another in silent horror. The Fear Street woods, where they had found Stacy. The woods, where— An image flashed in my mind from the TV news: the blue body bag lying in the muddy ravine.

If there were people in the room who didn't believe it before, they did now—we'd never see Simone again.

Rachel caught my eye. It was as if she wanted me to tell her this wasn't really happening.

I tried to be reassuring. But as horrified as I had been when Stacy had been found in the woods, it was nothing to what I felt now. This was Simone, someone I had known since kindergarten.

Mr. and Mrs. Perry were walking toward us, Mrs. Perry carrying a tray of cookies, and Mr. Perry holding a pitcher of milk. Mrs. Perry bit her lip when she saw the police. Mr. Perry took the tray from her and set it down on the coffee table.

Robbie Barron reached out and took a cookie. Everyone stared at him. How could he eat at a time like this? He bit into the cookie, and in the silence of the room, everyone heard him chomp. He glanced around and saw everyone staring at him. He put the rest of the cookie down.

Just then the telephone rang.

We all jumped, as if we had just gotten an electric shock. Mr. Perry bounded out of the room. He came back a moment later.

"Just my secretary," he explained, grim faced.

"Okay," Officer Barnett said, taking a large black notebook from her belt hook and flipping it open. "Let's get started. We need any information that might be helpful in finding Simone. *Anything,*" she added firmly.

"Everything is important. Understood?" her fellow officer added, his eyes surveying us one by one.

I nodded vigorously, as if it were really a question that needed an answer. Then Officer Jackson said, "Who wants to start?"

They stared at us. We all shifted uncomfortably in our seats. This was worse than when a teacher asked a question and nobody raised a hand.

A lot worse.

"Okay, let's start with where you all were last night," suggested Officer Barnett. She turned her eyes to the boy sitting closest to her—Justin.

Justin appeared very nervous, even more nervous than the rest of us. "I—uh—I was at—"

Why does he sound as if he's thinking up a lie? I wondered.

"I was at Elana's," he finally said. "Studying. I mean, you know. We were doing our homework together."

I stared at Elana. That was a shocker!

Elana caught my glance and blushed. She turned away.

Who asked who? I wondered. I bet it was Elana who asked Justin. She probably didn't like it that Justin had asked out Rachel and Dawn and passed her over.

I glanced at Mrs. Perry. But she didn't seem surprised. I guess she had a lot more on her mind right then than whether or not Justin was cheating on her daughter.

"I was working all afternoon," Rachel said, "at the Seven-Eleven. Then I was at home."

"I was playing tennis," Dawn told the police. She

glanced at me. I remembered her bloody tennis whites. But she had explained that, the accident with the fence.

Officer Jackson was looking at me expectantly. "I was working on the set," I began.

"The set?" he asked.

"Simone's school is putting on *The Sound of Music,*" Mr. Perry interjected.

The policeman nodded. "Go on."

"I already told this stuff to the police last night," I said.

"Tell us," Officer Jackson said patiently.

I told the whole terrifying story again. How I had stopped to find Simone. How I had found her room all torn up. About the blood on the carpet. And how I had run to the window for air and had seen a man running away in the darkness.

"Now," Officer Barnett said, "this is very important. Can you remember anything about what the man looked like? Anything at all?"

Everyone was staring at me. I felt myself begin to sweat. It suddenly seemed up to me, and me alone, to catch Simone's attacker.

I tried, in my mind, to stare out Simone's window again. But I couldn't picture the man.

He was a dark blur.

A dark, frightening blur.

I shook my head no.

"This sack he was carrying," Officer Jackson asked. "How big was it?"

I knew the question he was really asking. "As big as a person," I said.

Mrs. Perry gasped and raised her hand to her mouth.

"Robbie, what was wrong between you and Simone yesterday?" Elana asked tentatively. "I mean, it looked like the two of you were really having a big argument."

All eyes turned to Elana, then Robbie, then back to Elana.

"It was nothing," Robbie mumbled.

"It didn't sound like nothing," Elana said. "You were really mad at her for always showing up late for rehearsals. You said she was wrecking the whole production with her lousy attitude. You said if she didn't start coming on time, you were going to stuff her nun's wimple down her throat and—"

"Of course I was arguing with her," Robbie interrupted shrilly. "Who *didn't* argue with her! She was impossible!"

That word *was* made me wince. "Robbie!" I said.

We all stole glances at Mr. and Mrs. Perry.

Robbie blushed bright red. "Sorry," he said. "I didn't mean to—I mean . . ."

"Let's keep going," Mr. Perry said, stone faced.

After everyone had said where they had been the night before, Officer Barnett turned back to Justin.

"Did Simone have any enemies that you know of?" she asked. "Anyone who would want to cause her harm?"

"No," he said.

"And the last time you saw her was—"

"At lunch, yesterday."

"And she was—"

"Upset," said Justin. "Very upset, thanks to—" He glared at Robbie, who said, "Oh, please!"

Finally, after an hour of questioning, the policewoman snapped her notebook shut. "Thank you, all of you. If you think of anything you want to add, call us at the Shadyside police station. If we're not there, leave a message and we'll get right back to you."

Officer Jackson nodded to Mr. Perry as he and Officer Barnett headed for the door. Everyone in the room was standing up, ready to go. No one wanted to hang out a minute longer than they had to.

When I got outside, I was startled that the sun was still shining brightly. The Perrys' front lawn was green and cheerful. It seemed so strange after what we'd just been discussing. Everything *looked* fine.

I put my hands above my eyes to shield them from the glare. I watched Rachel head for her car. She was walking arm in arm with Gideon. Elana passed by me on my right.

"Horrible, huh?" I said. It was all I could think to say.

Elana barely looked at me before walking on.

"Wait a minute," I said, hurrying to catch up with her.

There was a long line of cars in front of the

Perrys' house. Elana was parked near the end, and I was right behind her. I didn't say anything till we got near my car. "I just wish there was something we could do," I said. "I mean, we were—are—some of her best friends and—"

"Listen," Elana said brusquely, "I've had it up to here with this, okay? I can't talk about it anymore."

She opened her door, got in, and slammed it shut.

Wow, I thought. Talk about not sticking together in a crisis. I stared after her as she pulled out. She was staring straight ahead and didn't even wave goodbye. Her face was frozen.

Then it hit me. She was frozen with fear. Just like the rest of us. And Elana's way of controlling fear was to pretend that bad things didn't happen.

I pulled out my rabbit's-foot key ring and fumbled putting the key in the lock.

Then I heard footsteps behind me—footsteps pounding along the pavement, running toward me.

And then I heard a voice shouting.

"I killed her! I killed her!"

chapter
6

I whirled around. Racing toward me was a stocky guy in a tan windbreaker that flapped behind him as he ran. His face was contorted in agony. His arms were outstretched, as if asking forgiveness.

"Very funny, Lucas," I said.

Lucas Brown was one of the weirdest kids I'd ever known. Even his last name, which is about as normal as you can get, was weird if you thought about it. Lucas Brown had short brown hair and brown eyes to match. And he usually wore—you guessed it—brown.

His eyes were set a little close together, so he seemed a little cross-eyed. That wasn't the half of it. Lucas once told me that he kept a diary of grue-

some deaths he heard about on TV. "Falling Crane
Chops Woman in Half"—that kind of thing. He
thought stories like those were funny. He said they
cheered him up.

Cheering up was something he usually needed—
in a big way. He was almost always in a black
depression. And why not? The guy had zero
friends. None that I knew of, anyway.

Right then he was laughing so hard I thought he
was going to fall over. "Gotcha!" he yelled.

What an unbelievable creep.

I turned back to my car door.

"Hey!" he went on. "I can't believe it. You really
believed me!"

I spun around and faced him again. "You have a
twisted sense of humor, you know that?"

"Oh, come on, Lizzy. It was a joke!"

"A joke? Simone has probably been murdered."

"I know," he said, his face darkening. I thought
he was upset about Simone, but then he said,
"Doesn't mean you have to give *me* a hard time if I
make a stupid joke."

I had trouble not screaming. "I don't believe
you," I said. "Can't you stop thinking about yourself? I mean, don't you feel even a little bit bad?
You used to go out with her!"

Lucas raised his eyes to the treetops. "Yeah, I
did," he said bitterly. "Thanks for reminding me."

He was standing really close to me. He grabbed
my arm and started to pull on me.

"Let's go get a Coke," he said. Lucas's magical

touch with girls: Don't ask—give orders. "I need to talk to you."

"No way," I told him.

He blinked. I could tell he was hurt. He said, "Okay, you're right. Now's not the time. Let's just go to my house and make out."

I pulled away from him angrily. My upper arm was aching where he had squeezed it. It felt as if I had just been given a triple booster shot. I stared at him as icily as I could. Then I got into my car and slammed the door.

He tapped on the window. He was smiling at me. It was a wicked smile, as if he knew something I didn't. I pushed the window button, and the window rolled down an inch.

Lucas bent over so his dark eyes were in a line with the crack. "Was that a yes or a no?"

He cackled.

"You really crack yourself up, don't you?" I said.

"I'm just so funny, I can't help it."

"About as funny as a rubber crutch."

It was the only insult I could come up with. I think I heard it when I was in the third grade. Someday I'd like to gather a whole bunch of really great insults. I'd use them all on Lucas Brown.

Lucas jammed his hand in through the open window crack and wiggled his fingers near my head. I pressed the remote-control button and shot the window back up.

With an angry cry Lucas quickly yanked his hand back. Then I peeled out.

As I drove away, I could see him, still standing there, still staring after me.

What a sicko! He's so crazy. I couldn't imagine what Simone had ever seen in him.

Then I remembered that Lucas was on the Shadyside High baseball team. He was one of the pitchers, and he sometimes played first base.

When Simone dumped him, Lucas was pretty bummed. He went around saying Simone had used him to get to Justin.

Lucas wasn't the only one who said it. Most kids agreed that she had.

It was easy to see why. When Simone started dating Lucas, no one could believe that she really was interested in him.

She did show up at every baseball practice— supposedly to be with Lucas.

Meanwhile, her visits gave Justin a chance to check her out. Simone wasn't subtle. She always wore her sexiest outfits to every game.

The minute Justin asked her out, Simone dropped Lucas like *that*.

I used to defend Simone when people said this stuff behind her back. But considering how messed up Lucas was, it made sense that she only went out with him to get to Justin.

I turned on the radio and searched for a soft, soothing song. Instead I heard "No break yet in the case, but the Shadyside police insist there is no reason to link the disappearance of seventeen-year-old Simone Perry with the recent deaths of Stacy Alsop and Tina Wales."

No reason? Sure. Except for the fact that it was obviously the work of the same psycho. I snapped the radio off.

Something was bothering me. Something stuck in my mind. Something I had begun to remember, but then forgot.

Lucas . . . Justin . . . Simone going to baseball practice.

Baseball! The team!

Yes.

The dark blur.

The running figure, carrying the gray sack.

The picture suddenly came a little clearer.

I pulled the car to the curb and tried to catch my breath.

I had just remembered something very important about the man I saw running away through Simone's backyard.

And what I remembered scared me to death.

chapter
7

"**G**uess who called me last night and asked me to the prom?" I said. "Lucas Brown!"

"*No!*" shrieked Dawn and Rachel.

We were in my green Toyota Tercel, heading for the Division Street Mall. It was a quarter to five on Wednesday night. Two long weeks had passed since Simone had disappeared. Two weeks with no call from any kidnapper. Two weeks that must have seemed like ten years to Mr. and Mrs. Perry.

I hadn't been able to stop thinking about her for a minute. No matter what I talked about now, she was there, like a dark shadow, following me everywhere.

"Tell me what he said, word for word," insisted Dawn.

"He said, 'Guess who you're going to the prom with? Me!'"

Dawn and Rachel both laughed at my imitation of his voice and abrupt manner. I wasn't laughing, though. The phone call had given me a chill.

"What did you say to him?" Rachel asked.

"I was very polite. I pretended he wasn't a creep. I said thanks, but I was still hoping Kevin would get permission to come. Which is the truth."

"And not only that, you think Lucas is a psycho killer," Rachel added. "Just what any girl wants for a prom date."

"You don't really think that," Dawn said to me. "Oh, come on," she said. "Lucas?"

"Hey," I said, "I just think he's weird, that's all. Everybody thinks so. And then, there's the jacket."

That's what I had remembered as I left Simone's house. The guy I saw running away from the Perry house was wearing a maroon satin jacket. Same as the Shadyside High baseball jackets.

Dawn's legs appeared in my rearview mirror. She was lying in the backseat, doing leg lifts. "Can't you two talk about anything else?" she said.

"No," I answered simply. "As a matter of fact, we can't."

"Okay," Dawn said, "so he was wearing a maroon jacket. That doesn't mean he was on the baseball team. Psychos are allowed to wear maroon too, you know."

"Yeah, but don't you see?" I removed one hand

from the wheel and sawed the air with it to emphasize my point. "Lucas is on the baseball team. It's the one thing he has to be proud of, even though he almost never plays. He almost always wears that jacket."

"Oh, come on," Dawn said. "Why would Lucas Brown kill Simone?"

"Revenge. He's hated Simone's guts ever since she dumped him."

"Get serious," Dawn said. "People don't go around murdering people who've dumped them!"

"Lucas isn't just anybody," I reminded her. "He's a first-class lunatic."

"And his eyes are a little crossed," Rachel chimed in.

Dawn snickered. "Having an eye problem doesn't make him a murderer."

"Well, he's definitely on the weird side, that's for sure," Rachel said. "I heard when his parents decided to put his dog to sleep, Lucas went out and hanged it from a maple tree in his backyard."

"Oh, puh-lease," groaned Dawn. "Where'd you hear that garbage?"

"Gideon," admitted Rachel, blushing. I took my eyes off the road and glanced at her. It occurred to me that Gideon was on the baseball team as well. But why would—

Dawn sat up and broke my train of thought. "Look, Lizzy," she said. "You *know* who did it. So do I. So does everybody else in Shadyside."

Rachel's eyes widened. "Who?"

"The same madman who killed that girl from Waynesbridge and dragged her to the Fear Street woods," answered Dawn. *"And* the girl over in Durham. Now, why would Lucas kill *those* girls? Did they dump him too?"

"I don't know," I said. "Maybe he just wants to see himself on TV. He keeps a journal of strange deaths and murders, you know."

Dawn rolled her eyes. "Oh, he just thinks that makes him cool."

I thought about this for a moment. I guess I *was* overreacting. The thought of Lucas actually killing Simone did seem incredible.

"Maybe you're right," I said.

We were driving by school now. All the lights were out. The building loomed in the twilight like an ancient and evil castle.

Great—now even our school was scaring me.

I made a left at the light. Rachel turned to me, surprised.

"Hey," Dawn said from the backseat. "Division Street is thataway."

"I want to stop at Simone's," I explained. "See if there's any news."

Dawn complained, but I insisted. A minute later I swung the car into the Perrys' driveway and parked behind their big silver Lincoln. The porch light was on. I guess the Perrys were still praying that Simone would return.

Rachel went with me as I rang the doorbell. Dawn waited in the car.

Mr. Perry answered, more haggard than before. His white shirt and tie were rumpled, as if he had slept in his clothes, and a day's growth of beard darkened his face.

"No kidnapper has called," he told us sadly. He stared out over our heads at the car.

"It's Dawn," I explained.

He nodded. "Listen," he said, "I don't want to scare you, but at this point the police are considering it very serious. They say they could be dealing with the same man who—"

He stopped. He couldn't bring himself to say the word *killed*. Instead, he said, "The same man they're looking for about those other two girls."

His eyes met mine. It was as if the life had gone out of them. He didn't even manage a slight smile. "Get home safe," he told us and closed the door.

Back in the car Dawn read our faces. She didn't need to ask if there was any news.

As we drove on to the mall, Rachel said, "She was the best actress, you know? Really gifted."

"She was one of the funniest people I've ever met," I agreed.

"I can't believe the whole thing," Rachel went on. "That she's gone, you know? There's like this big, gaping hole in my life where a friend used to be."

I bit my lip. "It's true what they say. You end up wishing you had said all these things to her, before."

"Like 'I love you,'" Rachel agreed.

"Oh, barf!" was Dawn's response.

"What?" I took my eyes off the road to glare at her in the rearview mirror.

"You heard me. I'm throwing up back here."

I could feel the anger rising in my throat. "How can you be so insensitive?"

"Look," Dawn said. "What happened to Simone is a tragedy. I'm as sorry as you guys are. But let's not exaggerate. Simone was never my best friend. And if you guys are honest with yourselves, you'll admit she wasn't your best friend, either. She was incredibly self-centered. I mean, can you name one single thing she ever did for either of you?"

"Just shut up, will you?" I stepped on the gas. I could feel the back of my neck getting hot.

I was driving about twenty miles an hour over the speed limit. We rode in silence for several miles.

"Look—" Dawn started up again—"hate me if you like, but all I'm saying is that we should try to get this off our minds for a few hours."

"How?" I asked miserably.

"By going ahead with our plan. We're going to the mall, right? We're going to check out sexy prom dresses that will have all the guys drooling. And then we're going to catch a movie. And we're going to have a great time. Agreed?"

Rachel and I exchanged glances. I shrugged. "Agreed," Rachel and I both said in unison. But neither of us believed it.

Then Dawn clapped her hands together. "Hey," she said. "The prom is only two and a half weeks away!"

"Great," said Rachel gloomily.

Dawn said, "I've got to decide who I'm going with pretty soon."

True to her prediction, Dawn had already been asked to the prom by three boys.

"I wouldn't mind being asked by three guys," Rachel grumbled.

"Everyone knows you're going with Gideon," I told her, "so no one would ask you."

"Right," said Rachel.

"It's true. If you want offers, break up with Gideon. You'll get plenty of guys asking you to the prom."

"Great idea," Rachel said, rolling her eyes.

"What about you?" Dawn asked me. "What are you going to do if Kevin can't come?"

"Go by myself, I guess," I said weakly.

"Wouldn't you feel really sorry for yourself?" Dawn asked.

"No." I shook my head, feeling totally sorry for myself.

Dawn said, "I talked to Lisa Blume today. She says they've hired a great rock band, the Razors, to play at the dance."

I nodded without enthusiasm. I was picturing myself dancing all alone.

A few minutes later I was posing in front of a three-sided mirror in a tight pink prom dress. We were in Ferrara's at the Division Street Mall. The prices in this store were outrageous, but my mom had told me not to worry about money when I was picking out my dress. I turned to the left, the right.

"It's not flattering, if you know what I mean," Dawn sniped, trying to hide her amused expression.

I felt my face grow hot.

"Just being helpful," Dawn said. "Which I don't have to be, considering we're competing against each other."

I went back to flipping through dresses on the rack. Farther down the row I could see Rachel, holding up an ugly red sheath dress. She pointed at it and looked at me questioningly. I shook my head but smiled kindly. I wasn't going to be like Dawn!

"What do you want me to say?" Dawn continued. "That it looks great when it doesn't?"

I shrugged.

"Admit it," Dawn said, poking me in the ribs, "you know I'm going to win, so why don't you just stop worrying? It doesn't matter what you wear."

"Right."

"But it's true. I always win everything, and you know it!"

I stared at her in disbelief. She just didn't know when to stop. What was worse, she wasn't kidding around anymore. I could tell that she was completely serious.

Then I saw it. Black, with spaghetti straps and a plunging neckline. It was so sexy, I could almost imagine guys fainting over the dress even without anyone in it. "Oooooh," I gushed, pulling it off the rack.

"Let me see!" Dawn snapped, grabbing at the hanger.

"Hold on," I said. "I found it first."

But Dawn kept yanking on the dress. Other customers were starting to stare. "Lizzy, don't be *stupid*," Dawn hissed. "It would look so much better on me, and you know it. You're not tall enough for a dress like this."

She gave a final yank and pulled the dress out of my hands.

"Thank you," she said, smiling icily. "Hold these, will you?" She handed me the three dresses she'd already picked out and flounced off toward the dressing rooms.

I stared after her. I had only one question for myself—why did I bother staying friends with Dawn?

I was so angry, I wanted to scream. But I didn't. I didn't even say a word. I just let her walk off with *my* dress. Which made me even angrier, of course.

That's one of my problems. I never get angry quick enough. I never speak up when I *am* really mad. And then I feel silly bringing it up later.

I thought about Simone. What would she do if she were here? She'd scream at Dawn. For starters. Simone wasn't big on holding back. Then she'd probably start doing some funny imitation of how competitive Dawn was. Something that would make Dawn furious but the rest of us laugh.

My anger was starting to fade. In its place came a feeling of terrible loss. Simone would never, ever make me laugh again. Except in my memory. I couldn't take it all in, but it was true.

Simone was dead. The words sounded so strange, even when I said them silently.

I looked at my watch—twenty to six. "Rachel," I called, "we've got to go. We're going to miss the movie." Rachel looked at her watch and put the dress she was holding back on the rack.

"Ta-da!" Dawn burst out of the dressing room in the black dress and struck a series of sexy poses. I had to admit, she looked fantastic.

"Okay, Madonna," I said. "It's showtime."

Dawn bought the black dress—our only purchase. Then we hurried to the movie theater.

After we got our tickets, Dawn and Rachel went inside to get seats while I got popcorn. I stood in the line, trying to decide if I should also get some Goobers. Not if I wanted to look good in my prom dress, I answered myself.

I was so lost in thought over this life-or-death issue that I almost didn't notice who was standing in front of me in line.

Spiky platinum hair. A tight black tank top decorated with sequins. Incredibly tight jeans that showed off a pair of thin, sexy legs. Even from the back I knew who it was: Suki Thomas. Suki was very popular with the boys at Shadyside High. And they weren't exactly interested in her because she could help them with their homework!

She had her arms wrapped around the neck of her date and was giggling in his ear. "Get the ice cream bonbons," she murmured huskily.

Her date was laughing. As he pulled away so he could talk to the candy counter clerk, I saw who he was.

Justin.

When he turned and saw me, he blushed. I'll give him that much.

"Hey," he said as if he were really glad to see me.

"Hi, Justin. Hi, Suki," I said, trying to keep the surprise off my face.

"Hey, Lizzy," Suki said. "Are you as excited as I am?"

"What about?" I asked.

"I mean, just think," Suki gushed, "a new Christian Slater movie. Wow."

Justin had paid for their popcorn. "C'mon," he said, pulling her away. "I want to get good seats."

I couldn't believe it. I knew Justin had been going from girl to girl, even before Simone disappeared. He had been with Elana the day Simone disappeared. And Dawn and Rachel had each gone out with him too.

Simone wasn't around to get angry anymore, but somehow that made it even worse. She was lying dead somewhere, murdered, and two weeks later he was out with Suki Thomas.

I couldn't believe it. Dawn, Lucas, Justin—was I the only one who cared that a girl in our class had been killed?

I tried not to get angry. I really needed to enjoy this movie. I felt as if I'd been carrying around a giant weight ever since I opened the door to Simone's room that night. Dawn wasn't the only one who needed a release.

But the movie turned out to be really dull. Not even Christian Slater could save it. The couple in front of me made out most of the time, so it was really hard to see. And my sneakers kept sticking to the goo on the floor.

Most of the time I was too distracted to follow the movie anyway. The events of the past few weeks kept flashing through my mind. I just couldn't make them go away.

Nothing was unimportant, Officer Jackson had said. *Was* there some detail I was overlooking?

"I've got to get a drink," Dawn whispered, climbing over me. She stepped on my toe. "Sorry!" she called back.

I craned my neck to look for Justin and Suki, but I couldn't see them. I tried to pay attention to the movie. About ten minutes later Dawn still hadn't returned.

"What's taking her so long?" Rachel whispered.

I had forgotten all about Dawn. The movie had finally gotten a little interesting. Christian Slater was in love with an incredibly gorgeous spy.

"Beats me," I said. "Maybe she fell in the toilet."

Rachel didn't laugh. "I'm going to look for her."

"Okay, just try not to—*ow!*" Rachel stepped on my foot as she walked past. The same one Dawn had gotten.

Up on the screen the woman spy was gently caressing Christian Slater's cheek. "So," she purred, "you work for General Frick?"

"We're like this," Slater answered, holding up two fingers close together.

I got lost in the movie again. Until I heard my name being called.

I turned around and peered up the aisle.

I could see Rachel stumbling toward me through the dark theater.

"Lizzy! Lizzy!" she cried in a loud whisper.

"Huh?" I pulled myself up from my seat.

"Lizzy! Come quick! It's Dawn! Something terrible has happened!"

chapter

8

 My heart pounding, I stumbled up
the aisle after Rachel, who hadn't waited for me.
She had burst through the double doors into the
bright lobby. I followed a few seconds later, my
eyes adjusting slowly to the harsh light.

There was Dawn. She was lying on her back on
the red carpet, her legs sprawled out, as if she had
fallen from a great height.

She's dead.

That was my first thought.

But then I saw that there was no blood.

Kneeling beside her was a young, overweight
usher in a red jacket and blue tie. Standing behind
him was a nervous-looking middle-aged man in a
blue jacket, who was wringing his hands. He wore a
brass name tag that said Manager.

Dawn was unconscious. Out cold.

"Rachel," I gasped. "What's going on?"

Rachel's face was very white, as white as paper. "I found her lying on the floor in the back of the theater," she said, her voice no louder than a whisper. "They carried her out here."

The teenage boy from behind the candy counter now came running up with a cup of Coke. The manager took it and said, "Bring the first-aid kit!"

Suddenly Dawn moved her head. Only slightly, but all our eyes were instantly on her. I knelt beside her. "Dawn!" I said. "It's me—Lizzy!"

Dawn answered with a low moan.

"She must have fainted," I said.

"I guess," answered Rachel.

The kid from the candy counter brought the first-aid kit. The manager flicked it open and fumbled for smelling salts. He waved them under Dawn's nose.

She jerked her head back. "Oh, please," she muttered. "No. . . ."

She turned on her side, holding her head.

The manager stared at Rachel and me. "You girls have any idea what happened?"

The way he said it, it sounded like an accusation. I shook my head. "Dawn!" I tried again. "Wake up!"

Dawn's eyes flitted open, shut again, then opened for good.

Suddenly her head jerked around. "Help me!

Help me!" she cried, and then cringed away from us.

"Dawn," I said, "it's me. Lizzy!"

Dawn stared up at me as if I were from the planet Mars. Then slowly she focused on everyone else, as if seeing them for the first time.

"No one's going to hurt you," I assured her. Why didn't I believe my own words?

A new thought had occurred to me about what had happened to her. And it was making my heart pound.

What Dawn said next didn't calm me at all.

"Killer," she muttered. "The killer."

I looked up at the manager. "Call the police!" I cried. "And an ambulance."

The manager snapped his fingers at the usher, who hurried off. Dawn reached up and grabbed my arm. "No, no, no. I'm okay," she insisted.

She tried to sit up. The manager helped her. Her leather skirt had hiked about halfway up her long tan legs. I smoothed it back down for her.

Dawn reached her hand to the side of her head. "Wow," she said, "it really—hurts." Before she could finish the sentence, she had begun to cry.

The manager gave her a tissue, and she blew her nose loudly. "I was coming back from the bathroom," Dawn said slowly. "I had just walked into the theater. I couldn't really see because it was so dark, but I thought I saw some guy coming toward me. Then he hit me—hard."

"Did anyone come out this way?" I asked the manager. He shook his head. "So," I said, getting up quickly, "whoever attacked her must still be in the theater."

The manager shook his head. He was sweating and was obviously very nervous. "There are two exit doors inside the theater," he said.

The usher hurried toward us. "The cops are on their way," he announced.

"Good," said the manager.

"I don't really have anything to tell them," Dawn said meekly. "I didn't see who it was. Why don't you call them and tell them to forget it?"

The manager shook his head no.

We helped Dawn to her feet. She was a little wobbly and seemed dazed and terribly frightened.

She wasn't much better when two cops rushed in to question her, their walkie-talkies crackling with scary-sounding reports of a burglary and a fire.

Dawn repeated her story. The manager kept interrupting with comments about how he and his staff had done everything they could and how it wasn't his fault. The police assured us that it was probably just some jerk, and not a killer.

"Why would he hit me?" Dawn asked.

"For no reason," one of the cops answered. "There are plenty of maniacs in this world. They don't need a reason. The guy probably saw you, saw it was dark, and let you have it. Just for the fun of it."

One of the cops offered to drive Dawn home, but she said she'd go home with us.

"Okay," said the cop. "Then I'm going to stick around till the movie finishes and see what I can find." The manager wiped his forehead with the back of his jacket sleeve and said, "What I'd really like to do is give you all free passes for another show. Come anytime you like. Anytime at all."

Rachel and I exchanged glances. "Thanks," I said, taking the passes, but somehow I didn't think we'd feel like coming back very soon. Then the two of us helped Dawn through the lobby and out to my car.

It was chilly outside, and dark—too dark for seven-thirty. I couldn't see a single star. The wind was whipping against us, as if trying to push us back into the theater. It was about to storm. I hoped it held off till we got home.

Slipping behind the wheel, I glanced at Dawn, who was leaning her head against the passenger-side window. In the light of a streetlamp I could see the bump beginning to form on the side of her head.

What's going on? I wondered, starting up the car and heading toward Dawn's house.

Was it just some deranged creep who had hit her? Or did the person deliberately want to hurt Dawn?

When I got home, my parents had the porch light on, along with a living-room light, the kitchen lights, and the light over the garage.

My mom hurried in from the kitchen when she heard me at the front door.

"You're home early," she said with a big smile.

My parents are very security conscious. We live near the river. It's just about the nicest part of town. Very safe. When we all go to bed, my dad puts on the burglar alarm, and we can't go downstairs without setting it off.

We've never had any trouble. The only time it went off was once when my dad got up in the middle of the night and forgot. We found him standing in the kitchen, holding a glass of milk, a bewildered expression on his face, as the siren blared.

I knew that the murders of teenage girls had both of my parents as upset as I was. Probably even more so. This was certainly the most excited my mom had ever been to see me come home from a movie!

"You got mail," my mother told me.

I stared at the pile of letters on the hall table. On top was a long white envelope with familiar-looking handwriting. "Kevin," I said with a grin.

I waited until I was up in my room to read the letter. His father still wouldn't give him permission to come for the prom. His mom had been in a minor car accident and was wearing a neck brace. He had made a lot of new friends. (That didn't make me happy.) And he still loved me madly. (That made me very happy.)

I was going to write an instant reply, but I had to finish my homework first.

That turned out to be more difficult than I thought. After ten minutes my American history textbook was still open to the exact same page I had started on.

I was trying to read about Lincoln getting shot. But every time I read the first sentence, I thought about Dawn getting whacked on the head. Or about Simone and the horrible things that had probably been done to her. Or about the girl they found dead in the woods.

A flash of lightning zigzagged down outside my window. The thunder followed almost instantly. It was the loudest thunderclap I'd ever heard. I stood up and stared out the window. It was hard to believe everything was still standing. It had sounded like a nuclear bomb.

Lightning flashed again. I heard a light pitter-patter, as if a thousand mice were running over the roof. Then I saw the first big drops of rain hit.

Crack! A curtain of rain whipped against my window. I jumped back.

Calm down, Lizzy, I told myself. Take a deep breath.

I took a few very shallow breaths. That only seemed to get me more worked up.

The storm was soon raging outside. Sheets of rain now ran violently down my window. The wind howled, as if it were a beast demanding to be let inside my room.

I got into bed and pulled the covers over me. The comforter was pink and ruffly. I'd had it for years. But it didn't feel very comforting at the moment.

I climbed out of bed and went to sit at my desk. I took out a sheet of the stationery my dad had had printed for me. It says "From the Desk of the Amazing Lizzy" across the top, with a picture of a frolicking pig. Pigs are my favorite animal. Don't ask why. I've got a whole collection of pig dolls and toys.

"Dear Kevin," I began. "I don't know if it's been in the papers all the way down in Alabama, but some horrible stuff has been happening here in Shadyside."

I crumpled that up and threw it away. I didn't want to start right off with the bad news. Why didn't I just write, "Dear Kevin, Simone is dead."

I shivered and covered my face in my hands.

When I removed my hands, I noticed that the door to my room was wide open.

I gasped.

It was my dad. He stared at me in amazement. "Didn't you hear me knocking?" he asked finally.

"N-no," I stammered. "The rain."

"Oh. Sorry. I didn't mean to startle you." He seemed pretty startled himself. "Just wanted to see if you were up for a game of chess."

My father adores chess. He can't get enough of it—even though I always beat him. "Sorry," I said, "I've got more homework to do."

He nodded and smiled warmly. "Everything

okay?" he asked, pretending to be casual. But I could tell he was worried, just like Mom.

"Yeah. I guess," I told him.

"Simone's parents haven't—"

"They haven't heard a thing," I said.

He sighed. "It's terrible."

I nodded.

"Lizzy?"

"I'll be extra careful," I told him.

He sighed again. "If you change your mind about the chess . . ." His voice trailed off as he left.

I examined my face in the closet-door mirror. No wonder he was worried. I looked horrible—dark circles under my eyes, face pasty white. Simone's disappearance was so upsetting. Now the attack on Dawn.

My phone rang.

I practically jumped out of my skin. It was the loudest sound I had ever heard. As if it were screaming in my ear.

When I answered, all I heard was sobbing.

"Who is this?" I kept saying.

"Liz-zy," a girl's voice wept.

"Rachel? Rachel?"

"Ye-e-s . . ."

"Rach—what's wrong?!"

She was crying too hard to talk. Then she sobbed, "You've *got* to come over! You've got to *help* me!"

"Rachel—what *is it?*" I cried.

"Help, Lizzy—*please!*" she begged.

Then the line went dead.

chapter
9

*T*he rain was coming down so hard and fast, my windshield wipers were just about totally useless. As I sped to Rachel's house on Fear Street, I saw the world outside my car as one dark blur.

Fear Street.

I was driving to Fear Street at night in the worst storm I had ever seen.

But I had no choice.

Rachel was in trouble. Maybe in serious danger. I had to get there as fast as I could.

I could barely see the white line on the side of the road ahead of me. The rain continued to lash down. But I kept my foot firmly on the gas.

Pictures began to form in my mind. Terrifying pictures.

I saw Simone, alone in her house, alone in her room. The killer enters. He has a knife. He wrestles with her. Slams her up against the bookcase.

I saw it all so vividly in my mind's eye. Saw the knife plunge down. Saw her duck. Saw the books crash to the floor. Saw the killer attack again. Saw him stab Simone again and again. The blood spurting onto the carpet.

I shook my head to drive the horrifying pictures from my mind. But the frightening thoughts wouldn't go away.

Why hadn't I told my parents where I was going?

When the phone line went dead and Rachel was cut off, I didn't think. I didn't ask.

I just ran out of the house.

With only a thin blue windbreaker held over my head, I burst through the front door. Running from my house to the driveway, I had gotten soaked. Now I felt chilled to the bone.

The Fear Street cemetery suddenly loomed on my right, glassy and distorted through the sheets of rain. The rows of white, crooked gravestones seemed to lean toward me as I slowed the car for Rachel's house.

I saw a bolt of lightning streak toward the middle of a row of tombs. The thunder boomed almost at the same instant. This is the kind of storm that can rouse the dead, I thought, shivering.

I leaned forward in my seat, my face almost pressed against the windshield. I tried to peer through the rain as the wind pushed my car toward the slanting graves.

I gasped as I saw a shadow dart into the road.

I slammed on the brakes.

But not in time. I felt the car jolt. I felt a bump. Something was under my tires.

My throat tightened in fear.

"No!" I cried aloud. "No!"

That bump. That horrifying bump.

I knew that I had just run over someone.

chapter
10

With my eyes shut tight, I slid to a stop. Breathing noisily, I pushed open the door and stumbled out into the rain.

Who was it?

Who had I hit?

A streak of lightning lit up the road and made it brighter than daylight for a split second. Several yards behind the car I could see someone lying in the middle of the street.

I started to run toward the person, the cold rain thundering on my head.

As I got closer, I saw that the figure was small.

A child?

"Oh, please—please, no!" I screamed into the rain.

My hair was plastered flat, like a helmet fitted to

my head. The blue windbreaker was sticking to me. My jeans were soaked.

"No! Please—no!"

And then I was standing over the body.

It was a raccoon. A dead raccoon.

The middle of the raccoon's belly was a mass of raw meat.

The animal's dark eyes were open and staring at me.

A wave of nausea swept over me.

I looked away.

It was a good thing I did.

Because I glanced up just in time to see a car round the corner and come roaring toward me.

I screamed and toppled backward onto the curb.

The car roared past. I don't think the driver even saw me.

Slightly dazed, I climbed to my feet. Avoiding the dead raccoon, I started running back through the pelting rain toward my car.

Somehow, driving almost blindly, I managed to pull the car up Rachel's driveway.

There was no sign of trouble outside the house. Lights were on inside. I ran up the walk and pounded on the front door.

I heard footsteps approaching. The porch light flicked on, and Mrs. West peered out at me through the white gauze curtains. Her mouth fell open when she saw me. I guess I was a sight.

"Lizzy!" she exclaimed, flinging open the door. "Are you okay?"

"Where's Rachel?" I cried.

"Rachel? Upstairs in her room. What are you—"

I didn't wait for her to finish. I took the stairs two at a time.

It was dark on the second floor. As dark as it had been at Simone's house on that terrible night.

I stared at Rachel's closed door, the narrow strip of light shining out underneath. I didn't want to imagine what I would see inside.

I didn't want to open that door.

But I had to.

Taking a deep breath, I grabbed the doorknob— and pushed the door open.

chapter
11

"**R**achel!" I cried.

She was sitting on her bed.

In the pale yellow light from her bed-table lamp, I could see that her eyes were red and puffy, her nose runny. Wads of pink tissues surrounded her, and she had an unsoiled tissue in her hand. Her mouth fell open as I burst in.

"Are you okay?" I cried.

"No," Rachel replied quietly. "I'm not." She blew her nose loudly as if to prove the point.

"Were you attacked?" I said.

"Attacked?" Rachel's expression became bewildered. "Huh?"

I couldn't catch my breath. I was panting loudly. It was hard to talk. "You called—you sounded so

upset—then the line—it went dead. I thought
. . . I thought the *worst!"*

"Well, you were right. The worst did happen."

"What?"

"Gideon is—" She started to sob again. "Breaking up with me."

I stared at her in astonishment. "You called me
over here in this storm for *that?"*

Rachel looked stung. "I needed someone to talk
to. I tried to tell you . . . about Gideon. But I guess
the phone was knocked out by the storm."

She picked up the receiver and listened. "Still
out." She glumly tossed it back onto its cradle.

I turned around to see Mrs. West in the doorway.
"Rachel? Lizzy? What on earth is going on?"

"Everything's fine," we both called in unison.

There was a pause, then Mrs. West said, "If you
need me, I'm downstairs."

Rachel sniffed. "You're dripping all over my
room."

"Well, how about giving me a towel?"

She walked out to the bathroom and came back
with a towel that she tossed at me.

I said, "And how about thanking me for trying to
save your life?"

"Thank you," she muttered. She avoided my
stare, her eyes welling up with fresh tears. "How
could he do this to me?"

My heart was no longer pounding against my
chest. I felt angry at Rachel—but also very re-

lieved. I toweled my hair briskly. "What happened?"

Rachel didn't answer. When I removed the towel, I saw that her face was contorted by crying. She was crying the kind of tears that are so painful they're silent.

"Rachel," I said gently. "It's not so bad. I promise."

She turned over and buried her head under an old brown gorilla pillow her mom had sewn for her when she was a kid. Her sobs came in painful bursts. I sat on the bed and put a cold hand on her shoulder.

"Rach," I said. "Come on. What happened?"

"He's dropping me for Elana," she said into the bedspread.

"He's *what?*"

"You heard me."

"I don't believe it," I said. Rachel and Gideon had been going together almost as long as I could remember. If any relationship seemed solid, it was theirs.

"How did it happen?"

"I don't know!" she wailed. "They've been working together on a social studies project and . . ." She didn't have to describe the rest. "Elana," she said bitterly, raising her voice. "She thinks she can have anything she wants. But she can't have—"

She was sobbing again, even louder this time. She pounded her gorilla pillow with both fists.

"Easy, easy," I told her gently. I kept my hand on

her shoulder, but she was really starting to shake. I couldn't calm her down. Everything I said only seemed to make it worse. I probably should have kept my mouth shut and just let her cry. But instead I said, "Well, I know a good way to get revenge. Beat her out for prom queen."

Rachel raised up on her knees and jerked away from me. "Are you crazy?" she cried. "Gideon was the only good thing in my whole rotten stupid life. Who cares about being prom queen? I won't even have a *date* for the prom!"

"I don't have a date, either," I said. I suddenly felt like crying myself. I was remembering the day Kevin found out he was moving to Alabama. That day Rachel had sat on *my* bed while I cried.

I tried to think of something comforting to say. "I'll be your date," I told her.

"Terrific."

She finally pulled herself together a little and apologized for making me come out in the storm. I told her I'd call her in the morning and headed back to my car.

The storm was still raging as I drove home. But at least I wasn't terrified now, knowing that Rachel was okay. Her heart was broken, but compared to what I thought had happened, a broken heart seemed minor.

I ran into the house, pulled off my soggy windbreaker, and stood looking for a place to hang it. My dad called out to me.

Uh-oh, I thought. Here comes a major lecture.

I had run out at night and taken the car without telling them.

He called me into the den. I entered reluctantly, knowing I was in big trouble.

But to my surprise, he was sitting at his desk with a big ear-to-ear grin on his face. He was wearing his favorite ratty old red bathrobe, the one with the ships' anchors all over it. In front of him his computer monitor was on and filled with figures. He's an accountant and is always really busy.

"Did you hear?" he asked as soon as I entered the room. "They caught the guy who killed those girls."

chapter
12

I should have been overjoyed. But I felt my heart start to pound all over again. I was almost afraid to ask who it was. The image in my head was of a boy with brown hair and eyes set too close together—Lucas.

"It was on the news," Dad said. "It was some guy who escaped from the state prison."

I let out a long breath slowly.

"And Simone? Did they say anything about Simone?"

My father's pleased expression quickly faded. He shook his head. "There's no word on Simone."

I sat down on the black leather footstool. "At least," he said, "we can relax a bit now. The guy is caught."

"Thanks for telling me," I said.

I went into the kitchen and opened the fridge. I wanted a snack, so I opened the vegetable crisper. Not that I wanted a vegetable. That was where my mom hid the chocolate from my father, who was developing quite a paunch.

I dug out a huge Nestlé Crunch bar, poured a big glass of skim milk, and sat down at the yellow table. I know it's ridiculous to drink skim milk when you're pigging out on a chocolate bar, but I figured, why not cut calories where you can? Anyway, chocolate always helps me relax. I've read articles that say it's addictive and that it makes people feel loved. I believe it.

Gnawing on a big chunk, I turned on the small kitchen TV.

The ten o'clock news was on—the weather just finishing. "So, in conclusion, rain, rain, and more rain," said the grinning weatherman.

The anchorman smiled and turned to the camera. "Thanks, Tony. We may not be dry tomorrow, but at least we'll be feeling a lot safer. Repeating our top story, a man believed to be the Shadyside killer has been caught."

I lurched forward in my chair as they showed footage of the killer being led into the Shadyside police station.

Most people cover their faces when they're arrested and on TV. Not this lunatic.

He stared right into the camera. And smiled. He was missing several teeth; his smile looked black and rotten. He was short, slight, but wiry with tattooed, muscular arms—arms that had been too strong for Tina, Stacy, and Simone.

"What made you do it?" cried a reporter, reaching through the crowd and shoving her microphone in the killer's direction.

The police were trying to hustle him inside, and his lawyer was shouting "No questions!"

But the killer stopped and flashed that rotten smile of his. "Do what?" he asked with exaggerated innocence.

"Murderer! Murderer!" a woman was shrieking off-camera. The killer disappeared into the station, still smiling. He turned to give one last wave to the cameras, his small eyes burning.

I reached over and snapped off the TV. I was sorry I had seen it. Now when I pictured what had happened to Simone, I could picture the killer's face. That smile. It was as if he had been sending a message to me—"I'm still going to get you."

I went upstairs, brushed my teeth, toweled my hair dry all over again, then climbed into bed. I turned off the light and stared up at the Day-Glo stars I had stuck to my ceiling. Usually they helped make me sleepy. But that night they weren't working. Nothing was.

Was Dad right? Could we all relax a little now? Was it possible that this whole frightening episode was over? Those questions rolling through my mind, I drifted into a restless sleep.

I didn't sleep long.

I was awakened by a loud, insistent knocking on the front door.

I sat bolt upright in bed. I stared at the clock. It was almost midnight.

Was it possible that I only dreamt I had heard someone knocking?

I knew I hadn't. But I waited in bed anyway, hoping I was wrong. The loud knocking was repeated. I got out of bed, grabbed my robe, and started down the stairs.

My mother, tying her robe as well, met me at the landing. My dad was standing in front of the burglar alarm control panel, punching in our code number to shut off the alarm so we could go downstairs without setting off the siren and waking the entire neighborhood. We all exchanged frightened glances and then went down the stairs together.

Dad yanked the door open.

Standing outside in the rain was a grim-faced police officer. He looked past my father to me. "Elizabeth McVay?" he asked.

"That's me," I said quietly.

"Were you at Rachel West's house tonight?"

My parents both turned to stare at me. "Yes," I said.

"Well," the cop said, "I'm afraid I need to talk to you. You were the last person to see her alive."

chapter

13

"Maria's rosary," I said. I made a check on my clipboard. "The captain's whistle. Check."

I was in the prop room, making sure I had everything for that night's rehearsal. Trying to keep my mind on what I was doing was the hardest part.

It was Thursday night. A week had passed since Rachel's murder. A week that had passed for me in a total daze. I just tried to put one foot in front of the other.

Soon after I had left Rachel's house that rainy Wednesday night, her family left too. Her dad had insisted on taking all the Wests out for ice cream— never mind the rain or that it was nine forty-five.

But Rachel was so upset over Gideon that she had refused to go.

Mr. West asked her nicely, then he begged, pleaded, and even ordered. He isn't the most understanding guy in the world.

Rachel can be as stubborn as her father. There was no way she was going out for ice cream when her boyfriend had just dumped her. "I'd rather die than go!" she yelled at her father.

Of course, those were words her dad will never forget. And he'll probably never forgive himself for leaving Rachel at home alone.

Then again, he thought the killer had been caught. We'd all seen his strange, smiling face on TV.

So Rachel's family had gone out for ice cream without her.

When they got home, Rachel was there.

Facedown on her bedroom floor.

Stabbed to death.

"The picnic basket," I said out loud. "Check."

I lowered my head. Now I was remembering Rachel's funeral. I thought the whole school would have been there. But not that many kids showed up. Gideon came. I bet he felt pretty low. He sure gave her a nice farewell present—dumping her for Elana.

They buried her in the new section of the Fear Street cemetery. It started raining again during the ceremony.

I tried focusing my attention on the play. I used to love being up in the prop room. At our school the prop room is way up at the top of the flies—that's what they call the area above the stage. It's hidden in a corner at the end of the catwalk that goes across the stage. It's so small it feels like a secret attic room. It's filled with all kinds of wild props. There are cardboard boxes stuffed with swords, feathers, old-fashioned phones, canes, every kind of dishware, bells, whistles, even a gun with a flag inside that says "Bang!" when you fire it.

Right then the tiny cramped room struck me as very scary. Who would hear if something happened to me up there? No one.

Then I noticed something peculiar.

The door to a small closet was slightly ajar.

I knew I had closed it after the last rehearsal. I knew because I close all closets until they snap shut. It's a silly habit I have. I like things to be neat. I can't stand a drawer that's half-open or a cupboard door that's half-shut.

I slowly approached the closet. The only thing I could hear was my heart beating.

Slowly I pulled the door open.

A box of papier-mâché masks crashed down and almost clunked me right on the head.

There was no one in the closet. I knelt down and muttered to myself as I checked the masks. Luckily, nothing had been broken.

And that was when the boy's voice behind me said, "Hi, Lizzy."

I stood up fast. It was Robbie. He was pointing a gun right at my head.

"You're dead," he said.

He squeezed the trigger. The flag inside the gun popped out. "Bang!" it read.

"Very funny," I said. "You—nearly scared me to death. Then the joke would have been on you."

I tried not to let him see how hard I was breathing. But he was eyeing me strangely.

"So," I said slowly, "what do you want?"

He kept studying me for a moment. Then he said, "Oh, yeah," and pulled out one of the pieces of yellow paper that he took notes on at every rehearsal. "I forgot to give you this note the other night. The abbey flats are reading too dark under the lights. Could you lighten them up?"

"Sure."

Then a girl's voice said, "Can you fit one more person in here?"

It was Dawn, her long blond hair tucked up under her nun's wimple. She was the only one wearing a costume that night.

"Maria, aren't you supposed to be getting ready to go onstage?" Robbie said.

"Yeah. I'll go back down in a second. I just needed to check some of my props with Lizzy. I won't be late—promise."

Robbie crossed off the note he had given me and then inched around Dawn. "Hurry up," he called back as he moved along the catwalk toward the ladder that led down to the stage.

Dawn and I stared at each other. Something about her expression scared me. "What's up?" I said.

"This was a huge mistake," she said.

"What was a huge mistake?"

"I never should have agreed to take over Simone's part in the play. Never."

"Why?"

"Because it's just totally freaking me out, that's why. Wearing a dead girl's costume. Why don't I just wear a big sign that says, 'Me next!'"

I started to laugh but caught myself. "I'm scared too," I told her.

Dawn stared at me hard, as if she were trying to see right through me. "Have you been thinking what I've been thinking?" she asked.

It made me shiver. These past few days, a terrible idea had formed in my mind. Apparently, it had occurred to Dawn as well. "What are you talking about?" I said, pretending I didn't know what she meant.

"First Simone, then Rachel. And that guy who attacked me at the movies."

"Yeah? So?"

Dawn was still giving me that freaky stare, as if we shared a horrible secret. "Well, do you think someone has set out to kill off the prom queens?"

"The prom queens?" My voice cracked when I said it. "I don't believe it. Why would—"

"You think it's just a coincidence?" Dawn asked incredulously.

"Sure. It could be."

"It can't be!"

"Maria!" It was Robbie, down in the auditorium. "Places, please."

"Just a second!" Dawn called down.

"But they caught the guy who—" I began.

"Sure," Dawn went on, lowering her voice. "But he was already in custody when Rachel was killed. And he won't confess to killing Simone. Come on, Lizzy, it's pretty clear. Somebody else is after us. And I do mean *us.*"

Dawn's left eye twitched. I realized she was feeling as scared as I was.

I cleared my throat. "There are only three of us left. You, me, and Elana."

"So what are we going to do?" Dawn asked, her voice trembling now.

I shook my head. I had no idea. "Look—you'd better get down there," I said. What I meant was, *I* wanted to get down there myself.

She ignored me. "You know what the scariest thing of all is?"

"Scarier than some freak murdering us one at a time?"

"Uh-huh. The scariest thing of all is, it's probably someone we all know."

"Well, you've certainly changed your tune," I told her. "You said I was crazy when I said Lucas—"

I stopped cold as I thought of Lucas stalking me with those crazy dark eyes of his.

"I still don't think it's Lucas," Dawn said. "I

mean, okay, even if he had a reason for hating Simone, what did he have against Rachel?"

"I don't know." Then I thought of Mr. Meade's game. Maybe that was the way to find the murderer. Put myself in his shoes, imagine what he was thinking.

I must have looked pretty spacey because Dawn asked, "What are you thinking?"

"Dawn!" Robbie screamed from down below. "Let's go!"

If I were the murderer, I was thinking, Why would I kill off the prom queens one by one?

Then it hit me.

"The money," I said aloud.

"The money?" Dawn rolled her eyes. "What are you talking about? What money?"

"The three-thousand-dollar scholarship that goes to the winning prom queen. Maybe some guy wants to make sure that his girl wins so he can collect."

Dawn made a face. "Would you murder four girls for three thousand dollars? I mean, why doesn't he just rob a bank? That makes no sense at all. Wait a minute! I know! Maybe it's some girl who wasn't nominated and who's really bitter."

"I think the money makes more sense than that."

"Well, just remember—it's not a coincidence!"

"DAWWWWWNNNNNN!!!!!" came the cry from down below.

"I gotta go," she said. She grabbed my hand and squeezed it. Her palm was cold and sweaty.

"Here's your rosary, Maria," I said.

She clutched the beads. "I'll need them," she said. "I'm going to be doing a lot of praying."

Dawn hurried out. I followed her out onto the catwalk. As she climbed down the ladder, I settled myself on the catwalk and stared down into the darkened auditorium and lighted stage area.

There was Robbie. He was giving a little speech to the cast. "This show is going to be great," he told them. "Just the thing we need to start off prom weekend with a bang. But we all need to work hard. Remember, there are only eight days to go until opening night. Okay—places!"

I looked farther back into the auditorium. Who was I looking for? Justin? He had come to watch Simone, I reminded myself.

Then I saw him. All the way on the right. And he was staring up at me.

It was Lucas. Our eyes met. He smiled up at me. He made a kissing motion with his lips.

I looked away. The boy is a psychopath, I told myself.

Thinking that sent chills down my spine. I remembered our encounter outside Simone's. Lucas was so crazy, he didn't need a motive. He could be stalking the prom queens just for laughs.

I once saw a movie on TV where this unpopular high school kid set out to kill off all the cheerleaders, one by one, because the captain of the cheerleading team wouldn't go out with him. After I saw that movie, I couldn't sleep for a week.

What was Lucas thinking? No—I didn't want to play Mr. Meade's game with Lucas Brown. It was too scary.

I tried not to look back in Lucas's direction. But after a moment I couldn't hold out. I glanced back at him.

He was gone.

Dawn was singing a solo, really belting it out while dancing around the stage.

"Hold it!" Robbie interrupted her. "Mimi," he said to the pianist, "a little faster there, okay?" He trotted up onstage. "Dawn, sorry to stop you. You're doing great. But I want you to try for an even greater sense of freedom, okay?"

Dawn smiled at him, wrinkled her nose, and said, "Sure." Robbie put his arm around her. He turned to the rest of the cast. "Can you believe how well Dawn is doing on such short notice? How about a round of applause?"

The cast obliged him with loud applause and cheers. They were used to Robbie acting like Mr. Showbiz.

I stared down at Dawn. I thought taking over Simone's part was supposed to be freaking her out. So why was she beaming as if she had just won at Wimbledon?

Then I had a really scary thought.

Dawn had a clear motive for the killings!

She desperately wanted to win. She was crazy about winning. We all knew that.

Crazy. . . .

What if Dawn got some guy to kill the other candidates?

But what about the talk we had just had? She did seem genuinely scared.

I'd be scared too if I were responsible for two murders—with two to go.

So what about Elana?

No way, I quickly answered. I couldn't see her doing it.

I couldn't believe I was doing this. Suspecting my own friends of committing murder.

Without warning, another name popped into my head. It surprised me.

Gideon!

That day at Pete's Pizza, Gideon had talked about the scholarship money. He had even suggested the rest of us drop out of the running. And Rachel had told him he wouldn't get any of it. Maybe he decided it was time to switch horses. . . .

My head was swimming. Down below me they had started rehearsing again. Dawn was telling the Mother Superior about her confusion about Captain von Trapp. I had to hurry down the ladder and into the wings to lower the next set into place. I hoped I'd make it on time. No more daydreaming.

I carefully unwound the rope on my left. I made it just before my cue and let the rope go.

"Oh, no!" I cried as I realized that more than the set was dropping into place.

A big, heavy sandbag went plummeting to the stage.

Then I heard a scream from onstage.

It was Dawn's scream.

The sandbag landed with a sickening thud.

chapter
14

"Dawn!" I shrieked in a horrified voice I didn't recognize.

Kids on the stage were screaming as well.

When I got onto the stage, there was such a tight circle around Dawn that I couldn't see her.

"Dawn! Dawn!" I called, desperate to know if she was hurt.

Then I saw her nun's habit. She was standing up. She was okay.

I worked my way through the knot of people to get to her. I could see the heavy sandbag lying at her feet.

Dawn was crying. "It came so close," she was saying. "It came so close."

I put my arm around her.

"Lizzy!" Robbie looked furious. "What happened?"

"I really don't know." I stared up into the flyspace over our heads. "When I pulled the rope . . ."

I turned back to Dawn. Through her tears, she was giving me an accusing stare.

"Hey, it wasn't me!" I cried, hurt that she'd suspect me. "Dawn—don't look at me like that."

"Someone is trying to kill me," she said darkly, choking on the words. "And this is the second time they've tried."

"What?" Robbie cried with an expression of disbelief. He turned to the rest of the cast. "Okay, everybody, let's take five. C'mon. Give us some room."

He put his arm around Dawn's shoulders and walked her back to the dressing room. I followed. Dawn slumped into a chair in front of the big mirrors.

"Now, what's this?" Robbie said. "Who's trying to kill you?"

But even as he said it, I was wondering, What's Robbie really thinking?

Robbie had hated Simone. But why would he kill Rachel? Or his new leading lady, Dawn?

Stop it, Lizzy. Stop it right now, I warned myself. You can't suspect everyone.

"If we knew who was trying to kill us," Dawn said testily, "don't you think we'd tell the police?"

Robbie sighed. He picked up a powder puff, examined it, then dropped it back on the table. Then he turned to me.

I could see in the mirrors that I looked just as scared as Dawn did. "Now, what's this crazy conspiracy theory you've got going?" he asked us.

"Simone and Rachel were murdered," I told him. "Or did you forget that?"

"What is it with you two?" he said, pushing his glasses back on his nose. "I know these have been scary times. But no one's out to kill you. Obviously there's another psycho out there who got inspired by the first one. It's totally random."

"And that sandbag?" Dawn said.

"The sandbag? It was an accident."

I didn't like the way Robbie was talking. It made me suspicious again.

"C'mon," Robbie said. "I can't baby-sit you forever. We've got a show to rehearse. Now, let's go."

"Robbie," I said. "Someone just tried to kill her. I'd like to see how you'd react if that—"

"Lizzy, read my lips," Robbie said, his voice going up an octave. "It was an accident. Got it?"

"Look!" I said, surprised at how strange and shaky my own voice sounded. "Why are you being so dense? Dawn is right. This can't all be a coincidence. Someone *is* out to get her. Okay? And whoever it is, they're out to get me too. Maybe it's *you!*"

At that, Robbie threw his hands into the air and started to walk out.

"Robbie!" I yelled. "Two of the prom queens have died already. Okay?"

"Two of who?" he asked.

I couldn't take it anymore. I suddenly had to get out of there. I had to get out of there fast. I pushed him aside and stomped out of the dressing room.

"Where are you going?" Robbie shouted after me. "You have to run the scenery changes!"

"Someone else can do it!" I yelled back over my shoulder. I hurried through the auditorium, the cast members staring at me. I kept my head down and kept going.

I was about to burst into tears at any second. I didn't want it to happen in front of everyone.

I slammed out through the double doors. Then I started to run. The hallway was dark, deserted. The classrooms were all locked.

I shoved the metal bar of the exit door with my hip and was relieved to be outside.

It was raining. When was the rain going to let up? Maybe everything wouldn't seem so frightening and so dreary if it would only stop raining.

I ran through the rain to my car. Someone *is* out to get Dawn, I told myself. And that meant that someone was out to get me too. And Elana. But who? Who?

I clicked on my seat belt and screeched away, nearly hitting a passing station wagon.

Soon I was roaring down Division Street, my mind whirling.

"Oh!"

I cried out as a face popped up in my rearview mirror.

A hand gripped my shoulder from behind.

I screamed. And the car spun out of control.

chapter
15

*S*till gripping my shoulder, the guy in the backseat laughed wildly as the car lurched out of control.

My wheels slid on the rain-slick road. The car was skidding toward a guardrail.

I turned the wheels into the skid and pumped the brakes. That was something my dad had once told me to do when he was teaching me to drive. How I remembered to do it, I'll never know.

I hit the rail. There was a thud and scraping sound as my car fishtailed, bouncing along the railing. Finally I managed to get the car back on the road.

"What are you trying to do, Lucas?" I screamed. "Get us both killed?"

He let go of me and slumped back in his seat.

The road had widened now. I spotted a shoulder up ahead. Carefully I pulled over and parked. I was shaking. I turned around and stared at Lucas with total hatred. If looks could kill . . . I was trying to burn holes into him with my eyes.

He finally stopped laughing and his expression darkened. "Sorry," he said. "I didn't mean to scare you." He chuckled some more. "But you have to admit I gave you a jolt."

I didn't reply. I just kept glaring at him.

"Sorry, sorry, sorry," he said in a singsong voice.

"Get out," I told him.

"Aw," he said, "don't be like that. It was just a joke."

"Lucas, did you notice I'm not laughing?" I snapped angrily.

He frowned, bit his lip. "Listen—seriously." He leaned forward and put his hand on my shoulder again. I pulled away so hard I hit my head on the steering wheel.

"Keep your filthy hands off me!"

"Hey," he said sharply, "what's the matter with you? You act like I have a disease or something!"

I couldn't believe it. What a sicko. He was acting hurt. As if *I* were the one who had just nearly gotten us both killed.

"Get out," I repeated quietly.

Lucas's frown deepened. He wiped his face several times.

"Listen," he said, "this is crazy. The reason I'm here is because I want to apologize for being such a creep, and—"

"Well, you picked a pretty bad way to go about it."

"I know! I'm sorry," he said again. "But I knew you wouldn't talk to me any other way." He was giving me that serious, soulful look of his, but because of his close-set eyes the expression came out looking very scary.

"Listen," he said again, "what I'm trying to say is . . ." He gave me a nervous little smirk. "I'd like to get to know you better."

"Right." I rolled my eyes.

"A lot better."

"Forget it," I snapped.

"Why? Lizzy—I really like you."

I had heard enough—more than enough. I turned around in my seat, checked the mirror, and made a U-turn, heading back for school. I drove fast.

"Where are we going?" he asked.

"We're not going anywhere. I'm dropping you back at school."

He didn't reply.

His silence made me even more uncomfortable.

In the mirror I saw him slowly lean forward to reach for me.

"Lucas!" I yelled. "I'm driving!"

But his arms were around my shoulders now.

And then I saw it.

The arms around my shoulders were dark, purplish red.

He was wearing his maroon baseball jacket.

chapter
16

"Get out!" I shrieked, pulling out of his arms.

I screeched to a halt in the Shadyside High parking lot. Now I jumped out into the rain and opened the backseat door. "I mean it!" I yelled.

"All right, all right. Don't have a heart attack," he said.

He crossed his arms and smiled up at me. The unspoken message was "If you want me out, you'll have to throw me out." That was exactly what I felt like doing. I was rapidly losing control.

"Lucas," I said, trying to keep my voice steady, "I want you out of my car, now. If you don't get out, I'm going to start screaming at the top of my lungs. I'm going to turn you in to the principal and to the police. I'm going to get you in every kind of trouble I know how. Now, how's that for calm?"

Lucas flashed me what he thought was a sexy smile. "You're cute when you're angry."

"Out!"

He started to get out of the car. But very slowly.

I yanked on his arm, but he seemed to enjoy playing tug-of-war, so I stopped.

"There," he said, "I'm out. Now, what did you have in mind?"

I slammed the door behind him. Then I hopped back in the driver's seat and pulled away before I had even closed my door.

I caught a glimpse of the expression on his face in my rearview mirror. His smile had finally faded. He looked upset.

I drove fast all the way home. Too fast. I didn't want to get a ticket, but I needed to put as many miles between me and Lucas as I could.

I pulled into our driveway.

Funny, the porch light wasn't on. My mom almost always left it on for me. And my dad's blue Subaru wasn't parked out front. Must be in the garage, I told myself.

The rain had suddenly stopped, and the moon came out from behind a bank of clouds. I was glad for *any* light right then.

I bent over and grasped the garage-door handle. I yanked. It rumbled thunderously as it rose up over my head. The garage was empty. My parents were out.

Unbelievable. If there was one night I didn't want to come home to an empty house, this was it.

The door from the garage into the kitchen was locked. I fumbled for my key. I didn't have it on me. Only the front door key.

Then I heard what sounded like footsteps in the house.

My heart froze. I listened. Nothing. It must have been my imagination.

Standing as straight as I could, I turned and made my way out of the garage.

I put my hand down on something furry and jumped.

The old carpet my dad had piled on top of the boxes of junk he had stored out there, I saw.

The moon lit the walk to the front door. But the shrubs my father was so proud of, the ones that lined the walk, in the dark they loomed like huge monsters ready to pounce.

Get a grip on it, Lizzy, I warned myself. I had to try twice to put my key in the front lock because my hand was shaking so much.

I got the door open and immediately locked it behind me. I flicked on the hall light, and every other light I passed by.

The house was empty.

I breathed a deep sigh. And another. I looked on the hall table. No letter from Kevin. I hadn't answered his last letter. Still, I resented his not having written. Where was he when I needed him?

Chocolate. That was the next best thing I could

think of. I headed for the kitchen and my mom's secret stash in the vegetable crisper.

The kitchen light was already on.

Sitting at the kitchen table was Justin.

"Surprise," he said.

"Justin—how did you get in?" I suddenly felt terrified. He had the strangest grin on his face.

"Your parents *let* me in. How do you *think* I got in?"

"Where are my parents?" I asked, not moving from the doorway.

"They went to pick up your aunt at the airport."

"My aunt?"

My first thought was that he was lying, my second that I should run out of the house screaming my head off. Then I remembered this was Thursday. Aunt Rena was flying in from Dallas. I had totally forgotten about her.

"Sorry," I said with a sigh. "I-I've had a very tough day."

"It's been a tough time for all of us," Justin said soothingly.

I nodded my head. "Understatement of the year award goes to Justin Stiles."

I opened the fridge and stared inside. I took out a Ring-Ding. "Want one?"

He gestured at the plate in front of him and grinned. From the crumbs I could see that he had polished off the last of Mom's carrot cake.

His grin spread. His perfect blue eyes were twinkling. He was *so* handsome!

As scared as I was feeling, I couldn't help noticing that. Justin had what Elana called "whip appeal." His looks zapped you, like someone had just flicked you with a whip.

"Listen," he said, "the reason I came by—"

"You mean you didn't just come for my mom's carrot cake? She'll be hurt!"

I was starting to feel a little better. I sat down, across from him.

"The reason I came by," he started again, "is about Suki."

I waited, puzzled.

"I wanted to ask you not to say anything."

"About what?"

"About the fact that I was with her at the movies that night."

I thought about this for a moment. "What do you care?" I asked him, once I had swallowed a mouthful of Ring-Ding.

"The thing is, I don't want to go out with her again," he explained. "And I don't want it to get around that I went out with her and dropped her. She's got a bad enough rep as it is."

I rolled my eyes. I didn't believe him. But Justin was giving me that puppy-dog expression of his.

"You know, it's been pretty lonely without Simone around," he said.

"Lonely?" That didn't seem like the right word when your girlfriend had just been murdered.

Justin got to his feet. He moved around the kitchen, glanced out the window, then came back and stood behind me. I scooted my chair to the side so I could look up at him. "Yes, lonely," he said. "It hurts so much with Simone gone."

Justin reached out and gently cupped my cheek. Then he moved his hand and rubbed my neck. I pulled my head back and studied him warily.

"Come on, Lizzy," he said softly. "You're interested in me. I can tell."

I snorted. He looked stunned.

"Sorry," I said, "but I swear you're the biggest egomaniac in the history of Shadyside. What makes you think I'm interested in you?"

Justin's eyes widened. His mouth went slack. "Well, if you're not, you're the first girl I've met around here who isn't."

I got out of my chair and moved away from him. "I guess you're not used to being rejected, are you?"

"As a matter of fact"—Justin's back arched a little—"no."

"No," I agreed. "No one rejected you even while you were going steady with Simone."

"What's that supposed to mean?"

"What do you think it means? It means you were going out with Simone's friends behind her back."

"That's a lie."

I felt a surge of anger. "Don't call me a liar, Justin. You're the liar. You went out with Dawn. You went out with Rachel. And with Elana. And those are only the ones I know about."

"I don't know what you're talking about," he

said. There was a new look in those blue eyes now. Fear.

"You were with Elana the day Simone was killed," I went on. "You already told the cops that part. Or did you forget?"

"So what?" Justin said. "That doesn't make me a murderer."

I held my breath. "I never said anything about your being a murderer," I said finally.

"Well . . . then . . . what are you getting at?"

He seemed totally flustered now.

"Just that it was a pretty crummy thing to do to Simone," I continued.

"Well, I don't want to talk about that right now," he said, his eyes flashing. "And if I were you, I wouldn't talk about it, either."

He spun on his heels and walked out.

That was a threat.

I had just been threatened.

What would he do if I didn't keep my mouth shut? I wondered.

As if in answer, the front door slammed shut.

The five prom queen candidates—even Simone and Rachel—were all parading onstage in their gorgeous prom dresses. All the dresses were identical. They were all bright red. All the girls stopped with their backs to the audience.

Mr. Sewall, the principal, was standing at the microphone, holding a small white envelope in his left hand. Next to him stood Lisa Blume, the student council president. She was holding the queen's crown and scepter.

"And now," said the principal, "this year's winner and Shadyside's prom queen . . ."

He ripped open the envelope. All the kids at the prom had stopped dancing and were watching the prom queens. Mr. Sewall too. What he saw was so horrifying that he never announced the winner.

One by one the prom queens slowly turned to face the audience.

And as each girl turned, screams rang out through the auditorium.

Each face was revealed. Each face greeted the screams with blank and staring eyes.

The flesh on the girls' faces was decaying. Their hair was matted with wet dirt and dead brown leaves. Their faces looked as if they'd been buried in wet earth for several weeks. Bone poked through the putrid, sagging chunks of greenish flesh.

Simone's face was the most frightening. The flesh of her cheeks had rotted so badly that her cheekbones were sticking right through.

Only the eyes of the prom queens remained intact. The girls' eyes were all blood red; they stared at the audience with unblinking fury.

Ghoulish faces. In beautiful gowns.

The five prom queens stepped toward the audience, staggering forward stiffly.

Closer. Closer.

Until the smell of rotting flesh choked everyone in the gym.

The girls all raised their heads in silent, hideous laughter.

And as they raised their heads, their blood red eyes flaring, their necks were revealed. Their necks, their shoulders were covered with slithering white worms.

I woke up screaming.

I screamed so loud I also woke up my parents and my aunt Rena.

All three of them came bursting into my bedroom, their still sleep-filled faces tense with alarm.

"Sweetheart," my mother said, plopping down on the side of my bed, "you almost gave me a heart attack."

"Bad dreams are just bad dreams," my father said, patting me on the head.

He'd been saying the same thing to me since I was four. I didn't mind. If I ever have kids of my own, I'll probably tell them the exact same thing.

If only the nightmares would go away.

If only I could sleep one night without being reminded of my lost friends.

My parents and my aunt went quietly back to their rooms. I stared up at the ceiling, trying to erase the worm-covered prom queens from my memory.

The next day at assembly I'd have to give my speech for prom queen. I forced myself to go over in my mind what I had worked out to say. I was going to talk about Rachel and Simone.

"The two people you should vote for aren't here

today," I planned to start. "Rachel West and Simone Perry."

But as soon as I said their names, I saw their faces. Not the way they had actually been, but the way they were in my dream.

Just a dream, Lizzy, I told myself once more.

Just a dream.

Wipe it away. Away.

Of course, this one time my dad was wrong. This one time a bad dream was not just a bad dream.

This time the dream was real.

chapter
17

"**Y**uck! What's *that?*" I asked.

I was staring into a steamtable container of baked muck. I could make out yellow kernels of corn, old spaghetti, mashed potatoes that had gotten stiff, greasy hamburger meat, pale green peas, and a little of every other awful meal the school had served us during the week.

"It's shepherd's pie," Mrs. Liston, the cafeteria worker, told me with a blank face.

"Looks more like something the shepherd stepped in," cracked a familiar male voice in my ear.

It was Lucas.

I pushed my tray along without answering. I wasn't really hungry, at least not for shepherd's pie.

Lucas hurried to catch up. Steam rose from the

large glob of shepherd's pie on his plate. "Go on," he said, "take a taste."

"Lucas, for the last time. Bug off."

"Or else?" he said with that little smirk of his.

"Or else you'll end up looking like shepherd's pie," I said. There, I thought. My insults are getting better.

I paid for my container of yogurt and salad and headed for an empty table. Elana waved to me. She was sitting with Dawn. I nodded back but kept going. I didn't feel like sitting with them right then.

The prom was only eight days away, and there we'd be, the three remaining prom queen candidates, all sitting in a row at the table like ducks in a shooting gallery. Just waiting for some maniac out there to take a shot.

I found a seat across from some nerdy-looking freshman. He looked stunned when I sat down.

"Anyone sitting here?" I asked.

He was unable to answer.

"T.G.I.F., right?" I said, digging into my salad.

"Yeah!" he said.

He glanced down the long table. There were a bunch of seniors staring our way. When I looked back at my lunch date, he was puffing out his chest and smiling proudly. I winked at him.

For ten straight minutes he slurped on an empty carton of chocolate milk and told me how much he hated gym. "I'd like to kill that gym teacher," he confided in me.

I sighed. Even the freshmen were killers.

"Thanks for avoiding us," a voice said as I was finishing the last of my yogurt. I looked up. It was Elana, her face drawn, tight, and tense. I guess she was feeling the same pressure I was.

I stood up and said goodbye to the kid across from me.

"Yeah, see ya tomorrow," he said. I had made a friend for life.

Elana wasn't smiling. "Can we talk?" was all she said.

We had about twenty minutes left in lunch period. We decided to take a walk.

Outside, it was a pretty spring day. Thanks to all the rain, everything was lush and green. There were birds chirping, insects buzzing. You could feel everything beginning to come to life.

We headed for Shadyside Park, behind the school. Neither of us said much of anything.

We sat on a recently painted park bench.

"You ready for the assembly today?" I asked, trying to get things rolling.

"To tell you the truth," Elana said, "I've had so much on my mind, I haven't really thought about it. It's like I don't even care about it anymore."

I nodded and waited for her to go on.

Finally Elana said, "I just feel so terrible," and then she fell silent again.

I looked at Elana. She was wearing a long blue-and-white sweater over blue leggings and a gold band necklace that I was sure was real. She had her hair tied in a cute little ponytail with a white scrungie. On her cheeks I could detect just a trace of apricot blush.

She may have been feeling terrible, but she wasn't feeling so bad that she had stopped paying attention to how she looked.

Such cruel thoughts.

I scolded myself for being so harsh. Elana did look glum. "I just feel so guilty," she said, sighing.

"Why?"

Elana stared at me as if she didn't believe that I didn't know. "For going out with Gideon," she said. "For breaking him and Rachel up."

I avoided her eyes. I happened to think that it *was* really awful of her, but I didn't want to say so now.

"It wasn't my idea, you know?" she told me. "Gideon kept after me and after me. Said he really liked me and that he and Rachel were just meant to be friends. . . ."

She stared at me again. Obviously she wanted me to say it was all right. I tried but I couldn't force the words out.

"I never got to apologize to her before she died," she continued. "I—I just feel so bad about it. I think about it all the time."

Her eyes were getting moist. I had never seen Elana cry before. I suddenly felt sorry for her. I put my arm around her shoulder. "Hey," I said, "what happened to Rachel was not your fault. Stop thinking that way, Elana. We've got enough to feel bad about without blaming ourselves."

Elana gave me a grateful smile and swiped at her nose with the back of her hand. "Thanks," she whispered.

"By the way . . . has Gideon ever said anything to you about the prom queen contest?" I asked her.

She looked surprised. "No. Maybe. Why?"

"I was just curious. His family is about as poor as Rachel's, you know."

"So?"

I was trying to decide whether it was worth scaring her with my crazy suspicions.

"I'm glad we decided to go ahead with it," Elana said.

Mr. Sewall had called us in that morning—me, Elana, and Dawn—to see if we felt up to continuing the contest. Dawn had said that Simone and Rachel wouldn't have wanted us to quit, and Elana and I had both agreed.

"You have a dress yet?" Elana asked me, her eyes on a large robin, pulling a worm from the ground.

"No."

"Last night my parents told me I have to be home by eleven after the prom."

"Eleven?"

"I know." She shook her head. "Some prom."

"It's not turning out the way we thought," I agreed.

"Tracy Simon dropped out of the Halsey Manor decorating committee because she was scared to go out to the Fear Street woods."

125

"I don't blame her," I said. "I'm not looking forward to it myself."

Elana stared at her hands. "Do you agree with Dawn?" she asked quietly.

"About what?"

"That someone's trying to kill all the prom queens?"

I bit my lip nervously. "I don't know. Maybe."

Elana's face went blank. When she was scared, she just shut down. She smiled abruptly—a big forced smile—and stretched. "You know who I'm going with? Bruce Chadwin."

I knew she was desperately trying to change the subject. And she was succeeding. I gaped at her. "Bruce? Did he ask you?"

"Uh-huh."

"Dawn will kill you." I blushed. "I mean, she'll be mad."

"I know." She shrugged. "I always seem to be getting some girl angry at me. But what could I do? He asked me—not her. And it's not like she doesn't have a big choice of dates. And speaking of dates . . ."

"Kevin's father still won't let him come," I said. "I'll probably wind up going with my cousin Seth —the one from Waynesbridge. He said he'd do me a favor and take me. Is that the worst? But that's not my biggest problem. I'm really worried about my speech this afternoon. Do you think you could help me? I'm completely terrified of public speaking."

It's true, I am. In fact, I once read about a survey that showed that public speaking frightens some people more than death. I wouldn't go that far. But I do get really nervous.

I worried about it all afternoon. But the speeches went fine. We each got huge rounds of applause, and when Elana finished talking about why we had decided to go on, the three of us all got a standing ovation.

I drove home right after school. I had an early dinner with my folks and Aunt Rena. Then I headed back to school for play rehearsal. I wanted to get there early. Every time I tried to lower the flats for the captain's mansion, the back wall would stick about halfway down.

With only a week to go, Robbie was beginning to lose his sense of humor. I didn't need him screaming at me right then, so I wanted to get the problem solved before he showed up.

When I arrived there were only a few cars in the parking lot. The school hallways were empty, quiet. Whenever I passed an open locker, I banged it shut. I felt like making a lot of noise.

I breathed deeply. I knew that old school smell so well—a combination of floor wax, sweat, peanut butter, and sour milk. How could anything bad happen here?

Then I turned the corner and nearly bumped into Mr. Santucci, who was mopping the floor.

"Trying to scare me again, eh?" he said. He didn't smile when he said it.

The auditorium was nearly pitch-dark. Who had pulled the heavy curtains shut to darken all the windows? It must have been Santucci.

I made my way up the center aisle. It was the same trip I had made early that afternoon, to give my speech. But then the room had been packed, bright, and noisy.

Now I got an eerie feeling. And suddenly I felt as if I wasn't alone.

I walked up the steps to the stage. The act curtain was closed, so I felt my way along it into the wings. I walked slowly. There was plenty to trip on in the wings—ropes, props, lights.

That would be just my luck. A crazed murderer is stalking me. But I manage to avoid him. Then I trip and break my neck all by myself.

I found the master light board, felt the large wooden handles. I pulled down the first one and heard the huge bank of lights come on with a loud hum.

I pulled down all the handles, one by one.

I knew the lights were bathing the stage in warm color.

Then I turned around.

And started to scream.

chapter
18

Still screaming at the top of my lungs, I rushed onto the stage. I couldn't stop. My cries echoed off the walls of the vast auditorium.

As I approached center stage, the hideous scene became all too clear. Elana lay facedown in the middle of the stage, her left arm bent beneath her in a way an arm does not bend. The fingers of her right hand were stretched wide, as if she'd been clawing at the stage. Dark red blood had splattered several feet across the stage floor.

I kept screaming. Finally the auditorium doors burst open and Mr. Santucci charged in, still carrying his mop.

"Get an ambulance!" I screamed at him.

He stared up at me, confused. I charged to the edge of the stage.

"Get an ambulance—now!"

He dropped the mop, turned, and ran.

I was still onstage, huddled near Elana's lifeless body, when the emergency medical workers finally arrived a few minutes later. Two police officers bounded into the auditorium behind them.

I watched them all race toward me up the center aisle. I could hear their walkie-talkies crackling. By then I knew there was no reason for them to rush.

"Oh, no," said a woman in a white medical suit, the first to reach me.

"What happened?" barked a tall, red-haired cop as he came up the stairs.

Two paramedics gingerly turned Elana right side up.

I nearly fainted.

Her face was smashed and bloody. It looked like her face in my nightmare.

The first medic felt for a pulse in Elana's neck. Then he made eye contact with the rest of us. His face was pale. He shook his head sadly.

"Looks like she fell," one of the police officers said, staring up into the flyspace. She looked down at me. I recognized her. It was Officer Barnett. "Were you here? Did you see what happened?" she asked me.

"No."

The red-haired cop pointed up to the catwalk. "She could have fallen off that."

Officer Barnett leaned down and put a hand on

my shoulder. "Any idea why she would have been up there?"

I raised my eyes. "There's a little prop room up there," I told her. "I'm up there sometimes. She could have been—she could have been looking for me."

Officer Barnett started climbing up to the prop room to take a look around. I stayed down below and answered more questions from the policeman.

They were loading Elana's body onto a stretcher. I didn't know why they were taking her to the hospital. But I guessed they did that even if you were dead.

"She didn't fall," I told the cop quietly. "That much I know for sure."

"What makes you say that?"

I had no proof, I realized. It seemed so obvious to me, though. "I just know it," I said stupidly.

And that was when I saw it. It was clutched in Elana's hand. The hand that had looked as if it were clawing the floor.

Her hand was clutching a small swatch of maroon satin.

"And you say she seemed nervous?" Officer Jackson asked.

"Yeah. But why wouldn't she be?" I said. "I'm nervous. Dawn's nervous. We're all scared out of our minds."

My dad's arm tightened around my shoulder. He

was sitting on one side of me on our white corduroy sofa. Dawn was on the other. Officer Jackson and Officer Barnett were sitting across from us. Officer Barnett was taking notes.

It was after ten, and these questions had been going on for over an hour. It seemed as if I had spent the whole spring talking to the police.

Officer Jackson said, "But did she seem extra nervous?"

I sighed loudly. "Yes!" I was letting my exasperation show. "Wouldn't you be? I can't even sleep at night."

"Someone's killing off the prom queens," snapped Dawn. "It's so obvious."

Dawn had already told them her theory. Officer Jackson stared her down. "We're pursuing every lead" was all he said.

"I mean," Dawn continued, "I was excited when we were first nominated. Now it looks like we've been nominated to—to die! Can't you see that?"

Officer Jackson's frown deepened. "If you'd just answer a few more questions, then we'll be through."

Officer Barnett stood up. "I'm sorry, Lizzy. This won't take much longer. But you were the last person to see both Rachel and Elana alive. We're trying to find out everything we can."

She turned to Dawn. "Before the rehearsal, you were—"

"Playing tennis," Dawn said.

"And the last time you saw Elana was at the assembly?"

"Right."

Officer Barnett turned back to me. "Let's go over the part about the baseball jacket one more time."

I told her everything I knew. For the nine zillionth time I talked about the man I saw running into the woods, his maroon satin jacket.

"I'm telling you, I really think it's Lucas," I added.

Officer Jackson snapped his notebook shut and stood up. "We're going to talk to him next."

"So who do you think did it?" Dawn asked.

"We're following up every lead," Officer Jackson said.

Dawn and I stared at each other. "Why can't you at least tell us who your suspects are?" Dawn asked, her voice rising. "I mean, don't you think we'd be safer if we at least knew who to watch for?"

Officer Jackson shrugged. "Just take every precaution you can," he advised. "I'm afraid that's all I can tell you right now."

Dad walked the police to the door. Dawn stood up, stretched, and shivered. "Well, I guess I'll go home too," she said.

"What are you going to do?" I asked.

"Oh, nothing. Barricade my door, load my machine gun. The usual."

She gave me a little smile. I tried to smile back, but I couldn't.

"It's just us now," Dawn said.

"What do you mean?"

"For prom queen."

I looked at her to see if she was serious. She was.

"You're not still thinking about the contest, are you? Three murders aren't enough to get you to stop worrying about who's going to win?"

Dawn shrugged.

"Well, you win," I said. "I resign. I'm going to tell Mr. Sewall tomorrow. I quit. I don't want to be prom queen, believe me. Where are they going to hold the prom anyway? The Shadyside Funeral Parlor?"

I spun around dramatically. I meant to make that my exit line. But I bumped right into my mom.

"Hey, take it easy," she told me.

I walked past her and up the stairs without saying a word.

I went to my room and slammed the door. But I wasn't as angry as I hoped I'd be. I probably wanted to take it all out on Dawn. I couldn't.

I heard the front door close. I peered out the window into the darkness. I could make out Dawn, moving down the shadowy front walkway. She looked so vulnerable. I felt bad that I had gotten so angry.

I watched until I saw her car pull safely on its way. Then I watched for a while longer. I watched the trees swaying in the wind. I listened to the leaves rustle. If someone was out there, there were plenty of places for him to hide.

It wasn't until I sat on the bed that I realized my legs were trembling. I could actually see them shake.

I felt shaky all over. My chest felt all feathery.

I lay down, trying to calm down. I'm next, I thought.

It was a terrifying thought, but I couldn't stop myself. The words kept running through my mind: I'm next . . . I'm next . . . I'm next . . .

And then Lucas's words: I like you. I really like you.

I was still lying there twenty minutes later, my eyes wide open, one scary thought chasing another through my brain.

And then the phone on the bed table rang shrilly in my ear.

I stared at it, listening to it ring.

I didn't want to pick it up.

chapter
19

"*H*ello?"

"Lizzy?"

"Yeah?"

"It's Justin."

"Oh. Hi."

"Hi."

"What's up?"

"Uh . . . well . . . I, uh—"

He sounded nervous. Why would Justin be nervous? "What's the matter?" I asked.

"Nothing, nothing. Can I, ah, come over?"

"Come over?"

"Yeah."

"Now?"

"Well, uh, yeah."

"Justin, it's almost eleven. My folks have already gone to bed."

"Yeah, well, it's really important."

"What is it? Are you okay?"

"I'm fine. I'm fine."

"Can't you tell me what it is?"

"No," he said. "I'll tell you in person. Okay?"

Why did he sound so strange?

"Okay?" he said again.

"Yeah, I guess. . . ."

I couldn't think straight. Something was going on, but I wasn't sure what it was.

"Good. I'll be there in about fifteen minutes. I won't ring the doorbell, though. I, uh, don't want to wake your parents. So just wait downstairs, okay?"

"Okay."

Then I thought of something else. "Justin?"

"Yeah?"

"We can't. My dad puts on the burglar alarm at night. I can't go downstairs."

"Tight security, huh?"

"That's right."

"Well," he said, "turn the alarm off."

I heard the click as he hung up the phone.

The master alarm panel is on the landing outside my parents' bedroom. I could see the light under their door, but I didn't hear any voices. The light was shining under the guest room too, so my aunt Rena was also up. Hanging from the doorknob of my parents' door, my mom's cardboard sign read Alarm On.

I quietly punched in our security code. The red LCD light blinked twice, then faded out. I flipped the cardboard sign over so that it read Alarm Off.

Then I tiptoed downstairs to wait.

About twenty minutes later Justin's face appeared in the front window. He was wearing a maroon Shadyside High baseball cap. He pointed to the front door, and I went and let him in.

"Hey," he whispered when I opened the door. He gave me a funny grin.

"Come on in. We can talk in here."

I led the way into the den and closed the door. He leaned against my dad's desk and shoved his fingertips into the front pockets of his jeans. He crossed his legs. Uncrossed them. Then he took his hands out of his pockets. He seemed really uncomfortable.

"So," he said quietly, "you talk to the cops?"

"For hours. Listen, you don't have to whisper or anything. My parents are upstairs."

"Great," he said too loudly.

What was his problem? He was usually so laid back, so smooth. Now he was staring at me intensely. His forehead was all sweaty.

"These are pretty scary times," he said. "You must be scared, right?"

"You bet I am." Is this what he came over to talk to me about?

I looked down at his hands. So did he.

He was holding my dad's silver letter opener. The one with the curved handle and the dagger-sharp point. He started to pace, slapping his palm with the knife.

"So," he said, "what exactly did you tell the police?"

"Everything I could think of." I couldn't take my eyes off the knife. "I told them . . ."

I stopped myself midsentence.

"What?"

I didn't want to say.

"What, Lizzy?" he went on, his eyes boring into mine. "What did you tell them?"

What I was about to say was that I told the cops about the strip of maroon satin in Elana's hand. But instead I said, "What do you care?"

He laughed a crazy laugh. "You're right. I don't care a bit."

I wasn't looking at the letter opener anymore. I was looking at Justin's baseball cap. Sewn onto the front was the Tigers emblem.

Why hadn't it occurred to me before now? Justin was on the baseball team too. Not just Lucas.

Justin was all-state, one of the team's stars.

So Justin also had a maroon satin jacket.

"Why are you standing so far away?" Justin asked me, smiling awkwardly. "Think I'm going to bite you?"

"No, I—"

"Come over here, then."

My mind had started to race. "I'm happy over here," I said.

But Justin had started to walk slowly toward me, the letter opener held tightly in his hand. . . .

chapter

20

As I stood staring at the gleaming silver blade, there was a knock on the den door. It swung open.

"Dad!" I cried gratefully.

He was standing there in baggy, striped pajamas, confusion on his face. "Lizzy, who are you talking—"

He stopped when he saw Justin. He stared at him, then turned back to me.

"Dad?" I said. "This is Justin Stiles. Justin, Dad."

"Hello, Mr. McVay," Justin said. He set the letter opener back down on the desk.

"It's kind of late for visitors, isn't it?" Dad said. He smiled when he said it. He always smiled when he caught himself sounding like a parent.

I was so glad to see him, I didn't care about his sounding like a parent. I felt like hiding behind him.

"I'm sorry to bother you," Justin said. "There was something I needed to ask Lizzy about, and I didn't feel it could wait until tomorrow."

"I see," Dad replied, yawning. "Well, have you asked her?"

Justin looked at me, then back at Dad. "Yes," he said.

Asked me what? He hadn't asked me a thing, except about the police. My heart was still racing.

"Well, then, maybe you two can continue this conversation tomorrow?"

I laughed, even though there was no good reason to. "He's just leaving," I told Dad. "Come on, Justin, I'll show you out."

I ushered Justin to the front door, but he lingered there, refusing to leave.

We turned and looked back at Dad. He gave us a wave from the den doorway, then padded into the kitchen. I could tell he was rustling around in there, waiting for Justin to go.

"Thanks for coming over," I said quickly. "Talk to you tomorrow." I was talking loud enough for Dad to hear.

Justin stared at me. Finally he said, "Yeah. Tomorrow."

I watched him walk down our front steps, down the path, and disappear into the dark. Then I closed the door, locked it, and leaned my head against the door.

My father came out of the kitchen and stopped on the landing, staring at me.

"He left," I told him with more relief than he could possibly imagine.

My father nodded, then started slowly upstairs.

Had Justin been about to stab me?

Or had my overactive imagination taken charge again?

I was overreacting. I had to be.

Justin had certainly appeared nervous.

And he certainly had more on his mind than he was able to say.

But he couldn't have come over to stab me with a letter opener.

That was just plain crazy. Right?

I sighed. I hadn't realized how tired I was until right then. When you think you're about to get stabbed to death, it tends to make you wide awake. Now that I was relaxed again, I was exhausted.

I went back upstairs, brushed my teeth, got undressed, and climbed into bed. I closed my eyes and nestled into my pillow. I threw my arm around my second pillow for comfort—my favorite sleep pose. Maybe I could get a good night's sleep for once.

Tap.

My eyes popped open in the dark. I strained to listen.

What had I just heard?

Someone at the door? At the window? Someone trying to get into my room?

My chest was heaving as if I had just run a marathon.

Tap tap.

There it was again. And it was coming from the window. I reached over and flicked on my bedside lamp. Everything appeared normal enough. I got out of bed and walked slowly over to the window. I forced myself to look out, but with the lights on I couldn't see a thing.

Tap!

I snapped my head back before I realized it was just a tree branch, being blown by the wind.

Just a tree branch—but it looked like a skeleton's bony finger.

I slipped back into bed, and the tapping continued. It was as if the branch were beckoning to me, tapping out a message, trying to tell me something.

I was up all night.

I didn't go out all weekend. I spent most of the time in my room, lying on my bed. On Saturday night my parents and aunt were supposed to go to a dinner party, but my mom canceled so I wouldn't be alone. I objected, but not very hard.

Every time the phone rang, I jumped. I kept expecting it to be Justin. Dawn called instead. "I heard that Justin was at your house last night," she said.

"News travels fast."

"Some kids saw his car parked in your drive," Dawn explained.

Shadyside was such a fishbowl. Everybody was always watching everybody else and finding out your business. "Yeah, he came over," I admitted.

"I know *that,*" Dawn teased. "That's what I just told you. What I want to know is what he wanted."

"Good question. I have no idea."

"What do you mean?"

"Just what I said. I have no idea what he wanted. He gave me the creeps, if you want to know the truth."

He was giving me a lot more than the creeps—coming toward me with that letter opener in his hand—but I wasn't ready to start spreading rumors and accusing him.

At school on Monday I avoided him all day. It wasn't easy. I kept catching him staring at me. Once, between classes, I turned the corner of an empty hallway and almost ran right into him. "Hi," I mumbled, then hurried on before he could say a word.

"Hey!" he called after me, but I kept walking.

When I got home from school, I found a letter sitting on my pillow. It was from Kevin. I tore it open.

"Guess what?" the letter began. "Dad finally gave in. You've got a date for the prom!"

I was laughing and crying at the same time.

The prom. This Saturday night.

It seemed like such a long time ago that I had

even cared about it. Kevin didn't know what was going on, which made his letter seem even sweeter somehow.

I held the letter against my cheek. If only Kevin were coming sooner.

Now all I had to do was make it to Saturday. Make it to the prom.

Tuesday evening was the first dress rehearsal for *The Sound of Music,* which would be performed on Friday night. Everyone was tense, as they always are at a dress. Only at this dress everyone was *really* tense.

For one thing it was hard to walk around the stage without thinking about Elana. It was especially hard for me. I kept picturing how she had looked, sprawled facedown in the middle of the floor.

"Come on," Robbie was yelling, "let's get this show on the road, or we'll be here all night."

I was busy rechecking the props on the small table I had set up in the wings when Dawn came up behind me. Her heavy Pan-Cake makeup made her look very weird offstage.

"Has Justin tried to see you again?" she asked me.

"No."

Dawn stared at the stage, biting her lip hard. "Only four days to go."

"I know."

"I can't wait for the prom to be over."

"I know how you feel."

Dawn said, "Maybe we should bag it now and get out of town. Would Kevin let us stay with him in Alabama?"

I suddenly remembered—how could I have forgotten? "Hey, guess what? I have a date after all. Kevin can come."

For a moment the tension broke. Dawn whooped and clapped me on the back. "That's great!"

I shrugged. "I'm so frightened and upset right now, I can't really enjoy it. I mean, think about it, Dawn—if someone is killing the prom queens, there isn't much time left."

"I know," Dawn said, her eyes watering as she squeezed my hand.

"Places, everyone!" shrieked Robbie from the auditorium.

"Break a leg," I told Dawn.

"Am I sweating?"

"Yes."

"This stupid makeup," she complained. "It's so hot and it gives me zits."

Abruptly she reached out and gave me a hug. I could feel her heart pounding.

Then Dawn "Sister Maria" Rodgers hurried off to start the show.

"Okay, listen up," Robbie called from the auditorium when we were all set to start. "This time, no matter what happens, don't stop. We're going to get all the way through this show for once."

Then we began.

Dress rehearsals are supposed to go badly. It's an old theater tradition. "Bad dress, good show," actors always say.

If that was true, we were headed for one of the greatest productions in the history of Shadyside High. Everything went wrong.

Nuns kept entering at the wrong time. The reverend mother walked right into the captain's house in the middle of a scene. People dropped lines right and left and improvised crazy new ones. There were long, horrible pauses during which everyone on stage just stared at everyone else in bewilderment.

But Dawn was probably the most uptight. She kept referring to the housekeeper as the baroness and mixing up all the names of the Von Trapp children.

It was the first time we'd practiced with the band, instead of just a pianist. That went about as badly as every other part of the show. The musicians were either way behind the singers or far out in front. It was like a race where the lead keeps changing over and over again.

I made my share of bloopers, I have to admit. When Sister Maria quit her governess job and ran back to the abbey, I pulled on the wrong rope. A flat came flying in and almost beaned Dawn again.

When it was finally finished, Robbie called the whole cast onstage. "Okay," he said, "I hope you got that out of your system, because that was the worst production of *The Sound of Music* in the history of the theater."

"Oh, come on, Robbie," the freshman playing Gretel called. "It wasn't the *worst.*"

"Yeah, Robbie," said the captain, pulling off his fake mustache. "At least we made it through the whole thing."

"And we're all exhausted," the baroness chimed in.

"Okay, okay, sorry." Robbie came up onstage. "I guess I'm exhausted too." He took off his glasses and rubbed his eyes. "You're right," he said. "We'll pull it all together. I know we will."

He stared down at the pages and pages of notes in his hand. "You know what? You all deserve a break. I'm going to give these notes tomorrow. Everybody go home now and get a good night's sleep."

There was a cheer from the cast. Not much of a cheer. Everyone was feeling pretty tired. The actors all trooped toward the two dressing rooms to start slathering on cold cream to get all that awful makeup off their faces.

It always took me longer than anybody else to get everything squared away after rehearsal. First I had to hunt down all the props the actors hadn't remembered to return to the prop table. Then I had to take the props back up to the prop room. Then I had to pull up all the drop sets and make sure they were secure.

I was on my second trip to the prop room when I

noticed that the closet door was slightly ajar. I was positive I had left it closed tight. I hadn't opened that door since the last time I had noticed it was open.

So. . . .

So that meant that somebody else had been up there.

I froze.

And then a voice behind me said, "Hey."

It was Justin. He was blocking the doorway, leaning against the doorframe, staring at me with those pale blue eyes. He looked as nervous as he had the night before.

"So . . ." he began in a fake movie voice, "we meet at last."

"Justin—" There were people still there, I reassured myself. And if I screamed, they'd hear me.

"I don't know, Lizzy, call me crazy. But I've been getting the feeling you're avoiding me."

"That's crazy."

"But the thing is, I haven't asked you what I came to ask you last Friday night."

Should I make a run for it, screaming? There was about four feet separating us. Maybe he'd be so surprised I could break through.

Too late. He had started to move toward me slowly. His face seemed so tense. His hands were shoved deep in his pockets. Did he have a knife?

"What I wanted to know," he said, "is if you had a date for the prom."

I stared at him in amazement.

"Well, don't look so shocked. I know you're a little mad at me and think I'm an egomaniac and everything, but the fact is . . . well . . ."

"You're asking me to the prom?" I said.

He grinned sexily. "Right."

I began to breathe again.

"You're asking me to the prom?" I said again.

He laughed. "Well, yeah."

I laughed too. So that's why he had been so nervous! Nervous about asking *me* to the prom. I couldn't help it—I felt great. "I'm sorry, I'm not laughing at you, it's just—"

Justin came closer. "Hey," he said softly, "what do you say?"

"Lizzy? Are you up there?" a voice called up from the stage below. It was Dawn. I moved toward the door. Justin followed.

"I'll be down in a second," I called back. I shut the prop-room door behind me; then Justin and I moved along the catwalk.

"Uh, listen," I said quietly, "I can't go."

Justin's face fell.

"I'm sorry. I'm really flattered actually. But Kevin—I just found out—he got permission to come after all."

"Oh." Justin seemed really disappointed. "That's great!"

We looked at each other awkwardly for a moment. Then he said, "Well . . ." He went down the ladder first. I followed.

"Hi, Dawn," he said when he got down to the

stage. She was in black jeans and a pastel green tank top. I could see she had left plenty of makeup around her eyes.

"See you around," he told me and sauntered off as casually as he could.

Dawn was staring at me with fear in her eyes.

"What's going on?"

I smiled. I told her what Justin had wanted.

"He asked you to the prom?" Dawn beamed. "No! I don't believe it."

It annoyed me a little that she would be so surprised. "What's so strange about that?"

"Nothing." Dawn began poking me in the ribs. "So? So? What did you say?"

"I told him I'm going with Kevin."

She seemed disappointed and lost interest in the subject. "I forgot about that. So, are you almost done?"

"Five more minutes," I said.

She picked up my leather bomber jacket, which I'd left on a chair. "Isn't it a little hot for this?" she said, trying it on. "It's spring, remember?"

"Then how come I'm always cold?"

Roger Brownmiller, who was playing Uncle Max, came out of the dressing room and called to Dawn. "You coming?" He was the last person besides us backstage.

"I'm going to wait for Lizzy," she said.

"Don't get down on yourself," he told her as he left.

"Thanks," Dawn said. She watched him go, then

turned back to me. "You wouldn't believe how many people have been telling me not to commit suicide or anything. Was I that bad?"

"We all stunk," I said.

"Thanks a lot," Dawn said. She slumped out onto the stage. "Hurry up," she called, zipping my jacket up and down. "It gives me the creeps being here all alone."

I wish she hadn't said that. I had been concentrating so hard on the show that I had forgotten to be nervous for a couple of hours. Suddenly the fact that we were all alone in the semidark auditorium came home to me.

I remembered Elana. All the other bad memories weren't far behind.

"I'm almost done," I called.

I couldn't see Dawn now. And she didn't answer.

"Dawn?" I said. "Please don't play games. I can't handle it."

This time she answered me.

She answered with a bloodcurdling scream.

chapter

21

I raced out onto the brightly lit stage.
No Dawn.

Then I heard someone thrashing around to my right. I whirled around. It was hard for me to believe what I was seeing.

All the way on the other side of the theater, in the darkness of the wings, somebody was wrestling with Dawn!

"Dawn!" I yelled.

I started to run toward them.

Dawn and the man were fighting desperately now. Both figures a blur in the shadows. But I could see that the man had on a baseball cap and a maroon baseball jacket.

"Stop!" I screamed.

As I gaped at them, my mind went into overdrive. Who is it? I wondered. Who is fighting with Dawn?

The man was too slight to be Lucas. I remember thinking as I ran, "Justin?"

And then I saw a flash of steel.

He had a knife!

Dawn gasped as she saw it too. She and her attacker were locked together now, like some strange kind of statue. Both had their eyes on the knife. Dawn was trying to hold the man's hand back. With all his might the man was trying to bring his hand down.

The man was winning. His hand was slowly coming down toward Dawn.

Closer.

Closer.

The tip of the knife drew closer and closer to Dawn.

"No!" I screamed and raced forward.

And fell flat on my face.

I had tripped over a thick black lighting cable. I smacked down hard on the floor, the wood coming up to meet my head and cheek with the force of a baseball bat.

My head throbbing, I climbed dizzily to my feet.

Just then Dawn screamed again.

The killer had won. He had brought the knife all the way down and buried it in Dawn's chest.

I was too late. Dawn's grip on the killer's arm slowly relaxed. She collapsed to the floor and lay in an unmoving heap.

The killer stood there a moment, looking down at Dawn. Then he turned toward me. His eyes locked with mine. And then he stepped out of the shadows.

He was still holding the knife. It was stained with blood now.

Dawn's blood.

He stepped quickly toward me as I backed up on the brightly lit stage.

I finally saw who it was.

chapter
22

"Simone!" I gasped. "But we thought—"

"You thought I was dead," Simone sneered. "Sure—you all were *eager* to think I was dead, weren't you?"

"No—I—"

"But I couldn't afford to be dead, Lizzy. I had too much to do."

I scuttled back across the stage. She followed me.

"I staged my own disappearance," Simone said, her eyes flashing, her mouth twisted in anger. "I staged the whole thing. I knew my parents wouldn't care if I disappeared. And you want to know why? Because nobody cares about me. Nobody!"

"That's not true—" I began.

"Shut up!" she cried, cutting me off. She raised the bloodied knife, menacing me with it.

"My parents never cared about me. All they cared about were their golf scores and their martinis. Justin didn't care, either. He just used me. Nobody cared. Nobody."

I kept moving backward. "I don't understand," I managed to say. "Why kill the prom queens? I mean, it's not like you ever really wanted—"

Simone laughed scornfully. She took off her baseball cap and dramatically tossed back her long, dark hair.

"Prom queens?" she said. "Who *cares* about that? How stupid can you be? I'm not killing the prom queens. I'm killing everyone who betrayed me, everyone who sneaked out with Justin."

"But, Simone—" I began.

"Give up, Lizzy," she said. "You can't talk your way out of this one."

I had backed up all the way across the stage. I was about to step back into the stage-left wing. I didn't want to step into the darkness. But I had no choice. Simone was still coming toward me.

"I tried to make him care about me," Simone said, whipping back her hair with a violent toss of her head. "When I couldn't, I decided to punish him, to make him feel the pain I was feeling—by killing every girl he sneaked out with. I think he's figured out what's going on. At least, I hope so."

Simone laughed. "Wearing Justin's baseball jacket with my hair tucked into this cap, I looked just like one of the guys. Don't you think? You walked right past me at the movies and didn't even recognize me!"

"But where have you been hiding?" I asked, desperately trying to keep Simone talking.

"In heaven," Simone said coldly. She jabbed her bloody knife upward.

"I'm serious," I insisted.

"So am I," she said, grinning. "I've been staying in the prop room over the stage. It's really very cozy, and the cafeteria provided all the food I needed. Anyway, I'll be leaving soon. My work is almost finished. I'll make up some kind of story about being kidnapped and go home. You know what a good actress I am, Lizzy. Everyone will believe me."

She moved slowly toward me.

"What do you want with me?" I said. "I've never been out with Justin."

Simone laughed. "That's such a lie," she said. "It really is amazing the things people will say when they're scared." Her face turned furious again. "I was there!" she snarled. "I heard him ask you to be his date to the prom."

"Okay," I said lamely. "He asked me. But I said no."

"Is that so? Now, why don't I believe that for a single second? You're next, Lizzy. Sorry. I thought you were my friend, but you were only pretending. You didn't care about me, either. You're just like all the others."

My mind was racing. What was she thinking?!

Get in her head! I ordered myself.

Maybe she was thinking, I can't stop now. There's no turning back.

"Simone," I said, "when you're caught, they're going to put you away for a very long time. You know that, don't you? Why don't you stop now? Before you have more blood on your hands. You'll only make it worse."

Simone raised the knife in the air. "I'm not going to be caught," she said, "because the only one who knows my secret is about to disappear."

She started toward me again. I stepped back. But I was up against the cement wall. There was nowhere to turn, nowhere to hide.

Then I felt them.

The ropes for the drop sets were tied off right by my left hand. I glanced at them.

One of the ropes would bring down a sandbag right in front of me. But which one?

Which one?

I'd only have one chance.

Frantically I chose one of the ropes.

Taking a deep breath and closing my eyes, I yanked on it with all my might.

chapter
23

I opened my eyes as Simone charged toward me.

At the same moment the heavy sandbag plummeted down.

It was the right rope!

The bag crashed between us.

It landed with a cracking sound.

It took a long moment for the pain to register on Simone's face. Then she began to scream.

The cracking sound—it had to have been Simone's foot breaking under the weight of the bag.

Simone dropped the knife and fell to the floor, writhing in pain.

Crying out from the effort, she wrenched her foot out from under the sandbag. She reached out for her foot, but it was too painful.

She grabbed her face with her hands instead and lay down on the floor. She lay perfectly still.

The screaming had stopped.

There was total eerie silence.

I waited, trying to catch my breath. Then I moved slowly toward her. Was the actress faking again?

A few steps closer and I knew her screams had been real. Her foot was twisted at a right angle beneath her.

I grabbed the knife off the floor and pointed it at Simone's prostrate body. I was shaking, hysterical. But Simone didn't move.

She looked up at me, her eyes filled with agony and pleading. "The pain," she moaned faintly. "The pain."

Then she closed her eyes. Her head lolled back onto the floor. She had blacked out.

I stood staring at her for a moment before I came to my senses. Simone was going nowhere. Not with that foot. I ran across the stage. "Dawn!" I yelled. There was no answer.

But as I ran toward her, I thought I saw Dawn move.

"Dawn!"

I fell to the floor next to her, dropping the knife. "Dawn! We're safe! We're safe! Oh—please be okay. Dawn! Can you hear me? Dawn!"

Dawn raised her eyes to me. Then she opened her mouth as if to say something, but no sound came out.

"I'm going to get help," I told her. "I'll be right back."

"I'll wait," Dawn said.

I stared back at her, stunned. Had I really heard right? Had she made a joke? "You're going to be okay," I said.

I turned to go.

And that's when she got me.

Simone's face was just inches from mine. She squeezed her hands around my neck, choking me. Her long nails cut into my skin.

I didn't have time to scream. She dragged my head down. Choking, I fell backward, over Dawn. Simone was on top of me now, squeezing my throat, crying out from her efforts.

I tried to pry her hands off my neck, but I had no strength left in my arms. I was about to black out.

Suddenly Simone uttered a yelp of surprise. Her grasp around my neck loosened instantly. Choking, sputtering, I struggled to fill my lungs with air, holding my hands to my neck.

Still screaming, Simone crawled off me. I saw what had happened now. I saw blood pouring down Simone's leg. I saw the knife fall from Dawn's hand. She had stabbed Simone in the leg.

As I desperately tried to catch my breath, Simone dived for the knife.

"N-no!" I stammered hoarsely.

But Simone grabbed it, let out a scream of fury, and raised the knife over her head.

I was on my feet now. I dived at Simone. We fell

over with a crash, and the knife flew out of her hands and skittered out onto the half-lit stage.

We began wrestling, tumbling over and over. Simone grabbed a handful of my hair and yanked with all her might. I screamed and went down. As I tried to recover, Simone punched me in the stomach. Hard.

I curled up to protect myself. But then I realized she wasn't coming after me. She was hobbling away, out onto the stage, desperate to get the knife. Summoning my last ounce of strength, I lunged blindly and tackled her from behind.

She screamed again. "My leg! My leg!" This time the agony sounded even greater. But I didn't let go. I held both her hands behind her back as tightly as I could. And then I started to scream.

I was still holding her tight when Mr. Santucci finally ran in. His face was filled with alarm and disbelief.

I was still holding tight minutes later when the police and paramedics he summoned came rushing in.

Finally, as they gently urged me away, I let go of Simone. My clothes were soaked with blood—but none of it was mine.

I glanced over at Dawn on her back on the stage floor. She was still wearing my leather jacket. One of the paramedics quickly unzipped it, revealing her stab wound.

I gasped at the sight of it.

The medic glanced up at me. "It doesn't look bad," he said.

Dawn let out a relieved sigh.

"Can you hear me?" I asked.

Dawn managed to nod.

The paramedic quickly began taping on a large cotton bandage. "Looks like this jacket helped protect you," he told her.

I forced myself to smile at Dawn. "Hear that? It pays to dress warmly."

Dawn was as pale as a ghost, but she smiled back. "See you at the prom," she said.

chapter

24

Kevin held me close for another slow dance. I rested my head on his shoulder. The perfume of the gorgeous gardenia corsage pinned to my dress wafted up. When the music stopped, Kevin smiled down at me, his green eyes twinkling.

"I don't know about you," he said, "but this is one prom I'm never going to forget."

"That's for sure," I agreed. I had different reasons in mind than Kevin did.

We were walking hand in hand off the dance floor now, past the two bulletin boards the prom committee had set up in memorial for Rachel and Elana. Kevin caught my glance.

He said, "I think it's great what Mr. Brandt did, donating the prom queen money for a college scholarship in their honor." He took my hand. "I can't believe what you've been through," he said.

I looked across the vast ballroom of the Halsey Manor House to where Dawn stood talking to several cute-looking guys. We had abandoned the whole prom queen idea, but Dawn was still the queen of this party—she couldn't help it.

The music started again, and Kevin pulled me back toward the dance floor. I spotted Lucas Brown dancing with Shari Paulsen. Perfect—she was as weird as he was. But he looked happy for once. He finally had a date.

Moments later Dawn danced by with one of her many boys.

She stared admiringly at my dress. I was wearing the black, sexy one we had fought over at Ferrara's. Dawn had insisted I wear it instead of her.

"You know what?" she said, leaning close. "It looks better on you."

"You're just saying that to be nice, right?" I asked skeptically.

"Right," she replied. And quickly danced away.

About the Author

"Where do you get your ideas?"

That's the question that R. L. Stine is asked most often. "I don't know where my ideas come from," he says. "But I do know that I have a lot more scary stories in my mind that I can't wait to write."

So far, he has written nearly three dozen mysteries and thrillers for young people, all of them bestsellers.

Bob grew up in Columbus, Ohio. Today he lives in an apartment near Central Park in New York City with his wife, Jane, and fourteen-year-old son, Matt.

THE NIGHTMARES
NEVER END . . .
WHEN YOU VISIT

Next:
FIRST DATE

Fifteen-year-old Chelsea Richards is shy, lonely, and looking for love. She would give anything to finally go on a date. And soon there are two new boys in Shadyside, and *both* ask her out.

Chelsea couldn't be happier until the FBI informs her that they've tracked a violent, crazed killer to Shadyside . . . a killer who murders girls on the first date! Does Chelsea dare keep her dates? Will her first date also be her last?

R.L. Stine

Simon & Schuster Mail Order
200 Old Tappan Rd., Old Tappan, N.J. 07675

When the cheers turn to screams...

CHEERLEADERS

The First Evil
75117-4/$3.99

The Second Evil
75118-2/$3.99

The Third Evil
75119-0/$3.99

Available from Archway Paperbacks
Published by Pocket Books